METHOD OF MURDER

"Detective, how was Pia killed? I know Isaac found her body, but was she shot? Poisoned? Stabbed?" I paused in my assembly of the dry ingredients for pancake batter.

The detective tapped her hand on the end of the counter where she'd laid her tablet. "I hear you've acted as an amateur detective previously."

"Not exactly. I simply kept getting drawn into murder cases." I shrugged.

"I'll tell you the method, but first I'd like your word this time you won't get 'drawn into' my investigation." She surrounded the words in finger quotes.

"Fine with me," I answered. But was it?

"Ms. Bianchi was choked. Garroted, actually."

Garroted? "You mean with a rope or something?" A shudder rippled through me at the thought.

"It was actually a metal wire. We're looking into whether it was an instrument string, and if so, designed for which instrument."

"Wow. With thousands of musicians in the county this week . . ."

"Exactly . . ."

Books by Maddie Day

FLIPPED FOR MURDER

GRILLED FOR MURDER

WHEN THE GRITS HIT THE FAN

BISCUITS AND SLASHED BROWNS

DEATH OVER EASY

Published by Kensington Publishing Corporation

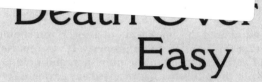

Death over Easy

MADDIE DAY

KENSINGTON PUBLISHING CORP.
www.kensingtonbooks.com

KENSINGTON BOOKS are published by

Kensington Publishing Corp.
119 West 40th Street
New York, NY 10018

All Kensington titles, imprints, and distributed lines are available at special quantity discounts for bulk purchases for sales promotions, premiums, fund-raising, educational, or institutional use. Special book excerpts or customized printings can also be created to fit specific needs. For details, write or phone the office of the Kensington sales manager: Kensington Publishing Corp., 119 West 40th Street, New York, NY 10018, attn: Sales Department; phone 1-800-221-2647.

ISBN-13: 978-1-4967-1123-6
ISBN-10: 1-4967-1123-8

First printing: August 2018

10 9 8 7 6 5 4 3 2

Printed in the United States of America

First electronic edition: August 2018

ISBN-13: 978-1-4967-1124-3
ISBN-10: 1-4967-1124-6

For Sisters in Crime,
the advocacy organization for female crime writers.
I would not be a published author if not for
what I've learned from my peers in this incredible group.

ACKNOWLEDGMENTS

First, my apologies to the Bill Monroe Bluegrass Festival, during which, to my knowledge, no one has ever been murdered.

I've loved incorporating colorful phrases for police lieutenant Buck and other characters to use in this series. Thanks to Betty Tyler, Ramona DeFelice Long, Kate Russell, and Max Carter for dialect help this time around. Tina Van Roggen kindly helped with clogging insights. The Sugar Cream Pie recipe is courtesy of Hoosiers Max and Jane Carter. With several fans tying for the win in a contest I ran, Celia Warren Fowler, Norma Bolling Wilson, Scott Forest-Allen, and Kristina Anderson came up with the clever campaign slogans for Chase Broward.

Nashville Chief of Police Ben Seastrom and Brown County Sheriff Scott Southerland were very generous with providing answers to my questions about police procedure in unincorporated towns in Brown County, towns like Beanblossom. Any mistakes are my own, and I promise that Wanda Bird and Anne Henderson bear no resemblance to any actual sheriff's officers, as far as I know.

Wearing her developmental editor hat, Terri Bischoff gave the manuscript a close read before I turned it in. The book is much improved due to her insightful comments.

My thanks to John Talbot, whose initial enthusiasm for this series turned out to be a great predictor of readers having the same reaction. Also many thanks to my editor, John Scognamiglio, and to the great support team at Kensington Publishing. The Wicked Cozy Authors continue to keep me sane (mostly) and inspired: Jessie Crockett/Jessica Ellicott/Jessica Estevao, Sherry Harris, Julie Hennrikus/Julianne Holmes/Julia Henry, Liz Mugavero/Kate Conte, and Barbara Ross. You gals are the best (and check out all those new names).

Once again, a big huge thank-you to my sons, my sisters, my beau, and my many author and Quaker Friends for supporting me in myriad ways. Love and hugs, always.

To cozy mystery readers and librarians, I continue to be delighted by how much you adore this series. Thank you! Please know that a positive review of a book you liked goes a long way to help authors. I would be ever grateful to see your opinion on Amazon, Goodreads, Facebook, and elsewhere if you enjoyed my story (and check out my other author names: Edith Maxwell and Tace Baker).

Chapter One

A crow scratched out a call from a tall black maple at the edge of the music festival seating area. A shiver rippled through me, but I shook it off. I don't believe in bad omens.

The bluegrass group onstage had finished with a flourish and a bow. The applause diminished and the buzz of voices increased as the musicians packed up their instruments and left the stage. I smiled at Roberto and Maria Fracasso seated in camp chairs next to me. My father and his wife were visiting from Italy, and what was a more American event to immerse them in than the Brown County Bluegrass Festival? Especially since Roberto had confided in me that he'd grown to love the twangy energetic genre when he'd been a visiting graduate student here all those years before.

"Abe is up next." I pointed to the stage with the giant American flag as backdrop. Above it stretched a big banner reading "Back Home Again in Indiana." My boyfriend Abe had just appeared, banjo case in hand. My guests had met him last night at the dinner

I'd thrown for them, my aunt, and her beau. Everyone had gotten along great. Actually, Roberto knew Abe from when he'd lived with the O'Neill family almost thirty years ago, but Abe had been so young he barely remembered the man who had been the Italian graduate student in town on a research grant.

"Roberta—no, I should call you Robbie," Roberto began.

"Either is fine." Roberta was my given name, after all, even though I hadn't known I was named for him until recently.

"Well, I am very happy." My father reached for my hand and squeezed it with his firm, smooth grip. "The weather, the music, but most of all to be with you. *Giusto,* Maria?"

She simply nodded and smiled. Even though Maria's English was about as bad as my Italian, the universal language of smiles went a long way. I was happy, too, getting to spend time with the father I never knew I had before last fall. And he was right about the weather. It was perfect. Early June, warm but not too hot, not yet buggy, with daylight lasting well into the evening. As crowded as the Bill Monroe Music Park grounds here in southern Indiana were, it was a good thing daytime highs weren't any warmer than the low eighties.

A petite woman in her fifties paused next to me at the end of the row of chairs. She wore a yellow festival visor on her cap of bottle-blond hair. Clipboard in hand, cell phone at the ready in a holster on her belt, she looked like she was in charge. I glanced at her face and recognized Sue Berry, a local woman who often came with her husband to my country store restaurant for breakfast.

"Hey, Sue," I said. "Are you working here?"

She looked startled, then smiled down at me. "I'm running the whole shebang this year, Robbie, if you can even believe it. Coulda knocked me dead with a flyswatter when they upped and asked." Her laugh was a peal of melodic notes that made you want to laugh right along.

"Somebody clearly made the right choice," I replied. "Everything seems to be running smoothly."

"I got a lot of helpers, but yeah, we're better organized than a marching band in the Super Bowl."

I introduced her to my father and Maria, and Sue leaned over to shake their hands.

"I don't talk no eye-talian," she said. "But you folks are surely welcome to our festival. Imagine, you came all the way from Europe to hear some of our hillbilly music."

Maria looked completely lost at Sue's local twang, and Roberto frowned.

"What is hilly billy?" he asked.

"Hillbilly means the traditional music of the people from around here, from Appalachia, from Kentucky and Tennessee," I said to the accompaniment of Sue's nod. "It's also called bluegrass, folk, or old-timey music." My Aunt Adele, who had lived her whole life a few miles from here, also used the term *hillbilly music.*

"Ah, I see." Roberto's frown slid away.

The amplified sound of instruments tuning up brought my attention to the stage. A fiddler with his hair in a knot on top of his head played a riff, then stopped to adjust the tuning. Pia Bianchi, a lanky woman with spiky red hair, a short denim skirt, and turquoise cowboy boots, plucked a banjo and turned the tuning pegs.

"She's got the nerve," Sue muttered under her breath.

"Pia does?" I asked. Pia and I had both joined a puzzle group a month ago, and so far she'd proved a little testy. Nothing major, but not a winner of the Miss Congeniality crown, either. I didn't know she played bluegrass, though, or I would have told Abe. Unnecessarily, as it appeared.

"The very same." Sue gestured with her chin. "Pia Bianchi. We used to be friends. Now she owes me a boatload of money and she ain't paying it back like she promised. I can't believe she's rubbing my nose in it, being onstage like she is."

Roberto gazed at Sue. "Did you say Pia Bianchi?"

"In the flesh," Sue answered.

"I know a Bianchi family back home. Their daughter Pia went to the States for college twenty years ago and never came home." He squinted at the stage. "I didn't see her since she was a girl, though. I don't know if this woman is the Pia from my town or not."

Maria tugged at his sleeve and an interchange in rapid Italian followed.

He faced Sue and me again. "My wife, she says this is the same Pia. She knows her twin sister, her . . . uh . . . Robbie, how do you say *perfect copy twin?*"

"Identical?"

"*Sì, sì, sì.* That is it. Maria says the twin looks like the one on the stage."

Sue snorted. "Well, I'd like to take and drag her

sorry butt off that there stage and make her pay up. That's what I'd like to do."

I'd never seen this side of Sue. Previously she'd always been a congenial diner in my restaurant or a grieving mother when one of her daughters had been murdered. Her annoyance with Pia was borderline angry.

Onstage, Abe stood facing Pia, both with banjos slung across their chests. Abe's fists were on his waist, while she held her instrument close to her body.

"No, we aren't going to do that number," Abe said, his ire clearly amplified.

"I wrote it and I want to play it." Pia's voice, also loud and clear, sounded defiant.

Did she know their mikes were live?

"We have six people in this group. You agreed to be part of it. It's not a solo act. What do I have to do to get you to understand?" His voice rose.

Abe and I had been a steady twosome since last winter, and I well knew it took a lot to push the normally easygoing, genial, caring man to the point of that kind of annoyance. So much that it almost never happened.

"Are you threatening me?" Pia asked.

"Of course not!" He turned away with a frustrated move, then twisted back to look at her.

"Hey, hang on, dude." The fiddler stepped forward and touched Abe's elbow. "I know Pia's song, man. It's totally good. She's got talent, man."

Abe shook his head. "No. We're sticking with the plan."

"Oh, for pity's sake," Sue rushed toward the

sound booth, a raised platform at the back of the audience area.

A young man dressed in black hurried across the stage toward Abe and Pia.

"Come on," Abe urged Pia and the fiddler. "It's time to start. We have the playlist we agreed on."

The stagehand faced the sound booth and made a slicing motion across his throat. I could see the worry on his face.

"Fine. Have it your way," Pia said. "But don't think I won't remember this. I can't be held responsible if something happens to—"

The amplification went dead.

Chapter Two

After things seemed like they'd calmed down onstage, I excused myself to visit the facilities. When I came out, I heard the rhythmic thudding and tapping of clogging. To the left of the restroom building was a wooden platform a couple of inches high. A banjo and a fiddle played as a man and a woman moved their feet in fast, tricky steps. The dance looked like a bluegrass meld of tap dancing and step dancing. I took a second look. The woman dancing was Beth Ferguson and the fiddler was her partner Ed Molina, a couple occupying one of my B&B rooms. Beth was a slender woman in a vintage dress, with dark anklets above lace-up black dancing shoes, her skirt swirling with her movements. The man dancing opposite her wasn't young and had a mature man's midsection in a blue sweat-stained dress shirt. But could he ever dance.

I watched mesmerized, my own feet tapping and twisting in place. Sue came up next to me.

"Aren't they amazing?" I asked. When she didn't answer, I glanced over at her. "Don't you like clogging?"

Her mouth twisted like she'd tasted a sour lemon. "I like the dance just fine. It's the dancers, or rather one dancer, I'm unhappy with."

"Why?" A ray of early evening sunlight slid through the trees behind me and illuminated Sue's smooth skin now marked by a furrow between her brows.

"Ms. Ferguson there? She snuck onto the festival grounds. Didn't pay her entrance fee. I don't know why she thinks she gets a free ride when everybody else here"—Sue gestured in a circle encompassing the grounds—"paid what they owed."

The music ended with a flourish and somehow Beth and the man seemed to know ahead of time. They ended with a dance flourish at the same moment. They joined hands and bowed to the sound of many hands clapping and even a couple of whistles and approving hoots. Beth extracted a handkerchief from her dress pocket and wiped her forehead. Sue marched toward her. I sidled up behind.

"Ms. Ferguson, I believe you owe us your entrance fee." Sue stood tall, which didn't get her very far.

Beth swigged water from a plastic bottle before answering. Ed joined her, fiddle and bow in hand.

"I told the person at the gate I forgot my purse and that I was on the program." Beth lifted her chin. "They said I could pay tomorrow."

"That's not what I was told," Sue replied. She checked something on her clipboard.

"It's true," Ed said, laying an arm on Beth's shoulders.

From the look on her face, Beth didn't seem to appreciate the gesture.

Because she was hot from dancing or because they weren't getting along? I had no idea.

"Look, we're both on the program for tomorrow night," Ed went on. "We'll bring the money then."

"See that you do." Sue set her free hand on her waist. "We have a lot of costs associated with this festival. We need participants to pull their own weight." She turned and hurried off.

Huh. Any time I'd seen Sue, she'd been totally easygoing. Tonight I'd seen her upset with two different people in a short time. The pressure of running the festival must be getting to her.

Ed and Beth murmured to each other. They didn't seem to have seen me, so I left, too, to rejoin my father and his wife. On my way back I sniffed the air. Somebody was enjoying a joint off in some corner. *Good luck with that,* I thought, spying a beefy security guard sniffing the air, too, his hand on his walkie-talkie.

The rest of the hour went smoothly with Abe's band playing tunes the audience recognized. People tapped their feet, clapped, and bobbed to the music in their chairs. A few couples even got up to dance on the dance floor in front of the seats. Pia apparently had recovered her equilibrium and played right along with the other musicians. Me, I had eyes mostly for Abe. I loved to watch this artistic side of him. His face was focused on the strings, sometimes glancing up at the audience and beaming his thousand-watt smile at us.

After the last number, we folded our chairs. Before we headed toward the parking area, I gave the stage one more look. Sue Berry had Pia cornered, and the conversation didn't look like a pleasant one. Sue gestured emphatically with one hand. If I hadn't known she was a Hoosier born and bred, I might have sworn she'd learned to talk in Italy. Pia crossed her arms and shook her head. I knew Sue and her husband were pretty well situated financially with Glen's thriving liquor store mini-chain. But why she would lend money to an Italian musician remained a mystery.

We made our way to the car Roberto had rented in Indianapolis two days ago, since my old van provided neither a comfortable nor a completely reliable ride, although it usually got me to where I needed to go. My father handed me the keys.

"Are you sure you don't mind going home for a bit?" I asked.

"It is no problem for us, Robbie. We will return this evening."

Which I couldn't do. I had prep to do for tomorrow, and my five-thirty alarm wouldn't ring any later because I stayed out late. "I'm glad. On the way home there's something cool I want to show you."

From the backseat Maria murmured to Roberto in Italian. He responded in kind to her, then twisted to face me in the front.

"Maria wants to know what the fight onstage was about, the one between Pia and Abraham. Can you explain? It was going too fast for me to follow."

"Pia wanted to play a tune she had written, and Abe told her they hadn't planned on it and hadn't rehearsed it." Seemed like a lot of anger from her for only one song, though. Abe would tell me what was really going on next time we talked.

Roberto thanked me and translated for Maria as I drove along the small roads of the unincorporated town, roads lined with the lush greenery of early June.

Five minutes later I turned onto Covered Bridge Road and slowed when we reached the eponymous bridge, barely wide enough for one modern car. The bridge was the picture of picturesque, with its faded red paint, a peaked roof, and two tracks of thick wooden planks to drive on. A yellow highway sign read ONE LANE BRIDGE even though anybody who attempted to drive through could tell at first glance. Above the entrance were the painted words *Beanblossom Bridge 1880*.

"It is safe to go across?" my father asked.

"Yes, it's safe." I crossed my fingers anyway. The sunny afternoon made the inside even darker and more mysterious as the car bumped slowly over the planks. Graffiti marred—or as some would say, *decorated*—the rough wooden walls. I didn't peer at it too closely in case obscenities were part of the scrawls. Once through, we could see Beanblossom Creek more clearly, full and rushing from the spring rains. I slowed to read a white laminated sign nailed to a tree trunk next to a wide gravel path.

I read aloud. "It says, 'Pastor's driveway. Keep clear for emergencies. Thank you.' A pastor is like a minister," I added, figuring my father might not know the term.

He laughed as his brown eyes lit up. "What kind of emergencies does a pastor have? An urgent lesson to the sinners in church, perhaps?"

I laughed in return but then became serious. A pastor could be called out on all kinds of sad emergencies—to comfort the victim of an accident, the family of a person who'd drowned, or to watch over any number of calamities that befell the residents of even such a beautiful place as Brown County, Indiana.

Chapter Three

I was starting to wonder if having bed-and-breakfast rooms upstairs from Pans 'N Pancakes, my breakfast-and-lunch restaurant, was such a great plan, after all. I'd wanted to utilize the unoccupied second floor of my country store here in South Lick. Since I already cooked breakfast for the public six mornings out of seven, adding *Innkeeper* to *Chef* on my résumé seemed like an obvious moneymaking plan. I'd done all the carpentry work and painting myself, skills I'd learned from my late mom. I'd hired out only the drywall, plumbing, and electric work. The Italians, plus several musicians with gigs at the festival, were my inaugural guests.

At times like these, though, all I wanted to do at the end of the day was put my feet up and work on a crossword puzzle. Having extra people in the building was a no-brainer in the not-too-smart category. Not my father and Maria. They didn't get underfoot. Right now they sat companionably at one of the restaurant tables, Roberto reading something on his phone, Maria making her way through a magazine. But the musicians had questions, wanted information, and were kind of a bother—of course in the nicest possible way. Ed and Beth had come in shortly after we'd gotten home. They waved and strolled arm in arm into the cookware area.

A minute later voices raised in the heat of emotion floated out. I grabbed a duster and edged closer.

"It just ruined the night for me, seeing her there," Beth said. "I shouldn't have to!"

"Babe, it's a public festival. You can't keep Pia from performing or sitting in the audience."

Pia?

"I want to go home. This was a stupid idea." Beth spit out the words like bitter pills.

Ed's voice lowered so I couldn't make out the words, but they sounded like murmured assurances.

"Okay. I'll stay for our gigs." Beth didn't lower her own voice. "But I'm not agreeing to play nice with that witch if I see her again. I can't forgive her. I'll never forgive her."

Wow. What had happened between Beth and Pia? The argument seemed to be over, so I scooted back to the cleaning closet and stashed my duster. By the time the couple emerged I'd washed my hands and was drying them.

Ed sidled up. "Where's the closest place to buy beer?"

"The gas station down the road has some, and the IGA out on the road to Nashville sells it, too," I said. "For more selection you'd be better off shopping in Nashville, though."

"Thanks," Ed said. "We wanted to check out Brown County State Park, too."

I explained how to get there. "It's a great place to go walking at any time of year."

"What about the best place to eat in Nashville?" Beth asked.

"There are lots of restaurants." I had to muster my inner patient self, or perhaps my long-suffering inner innkeeper, to politely list some of my favorite eating establishments until they went off on their explorations.

Talk of food had made me hungry, so I threw together a big veggie omelet for Roberto and Maria and me. I added a salad, a warmed sourdough baguette, and a glass or two of red wine each, and called it dinner. I cooked and served it in the restaurant, since seating in my snug apartment kitchen in the back was pretty tight for three. Strictly speaking, I wasn't supposed to serve wine in the restaurant except on a BYOB basis, but my establishment was closed to the public after three o'clock every afternoon, and I figured it was okay.

We were chatting comfortably, sipping the last of our Chianti, when the occupant of my third B&B room clattered down the stairs. I'd thought all the pickers and strummers would be out at the festival from dawn to after dark, but apparently I was wrong. The guest was Chase Broward, a slim older gentleman who had rented a room for the duration of the festival. He strode toward us, guitar case in hand, an easy smile on his tanned face, silver hair neatly trimmed and combed. Snaps gleamed on a black western-style shirt and the pointed tips of his tooled boots glowed from many polishings. He paused in front of the shelves of cookware, then approached us.

"Good evening ladies and gentleman." He smiled particularly at Maria, who nodded and smiled back with the briefest hint of sardonic playing at the corner of her mouth. "Ms. Jordan, you have an amazing array of utensils and devices. My wife would love this place. I'll plan to bring her over sometime soon, but I think I'd better purchase a piece to tide her over."

"Everything for sale has a price on it. Peruse the shelves as much as you'd like."

"Thank you. I'll do it before I check out. Well, I'm off to play some music, as we say in the trade."

"You're a musician full-time?" I asked. "I thought you said you were a Bloomington city councillor, Mr. Broward."

"I am, Ms. Jordan, but please call me Chase. I aspire to be in the music trade, but I might just have to settle for representing our lovely state in the United States Congress, instead." He beamed.

"Really? You're running for our representative's seat?"

"I would have aimed no higher than that, but I'm receiving a great deal of encouragement to campaign for the honorable role of senator, as it happens. Such a goal never would have occurred to me without urging from certain Monroe County Republicans. I cannot deny the call to a greater duty than my own."

"I wish you luck, Mr. Broward," Roberto said. He murmured a translation to his wife.

"Thank you very much. I'd best be heading over

to Beanblossom. You all are sitting out the music tonight?"

"I can't go," I replied, "but Mr. and Ms. Fracasso were planning on returning."

"You should ride with me, then." Chase looked at my father. "Please. Our country roads can be confusing in the dark, and I have plenty of room in my sedan."

Roberto and Maria exchanged a moment of silent communication, then he stood. "We should like to, how do you say, take you on your offer?"

"Take you *up* on your offer," I corrected. "Thank you, Chase. It's very nice of you."

"But I am afraid we might want to leave while the evening is still young," my father went on. "The jet lag, you understand, which you are not having. We have the GPS, and the days are long here. We will arrive back safely."

A wise move, come to think of it. Chase might want to stay out late jamming with the other musicians.

Chase nodded. "As you wish. I hope I'll see you over there, though."

"We shall look for you."

Maria nodded her agreement with her husband. She was a handsome woman with smooth unspotted skin despite being nearly sixty. Her wavy black hair was untouched by gray, and her eyebrows had a natural shape that started low in the middle then arched up and floated down. Roberto, on the other hand, made me feel like I was looking in a gender-changing mirror. We had the same brown eyes right down to the same smile lines around them. We had the same sideways curve to our mouths when we smiled and the same dark curly hair, although his was silvering at the temples and combed straight back from his brow. I couldn't get enough of looking at him.

A couple of minutes later they were all out the door and headed Beanblossom way, only a few miles distant. I let out a breath and upended the last bit of the Chianti into my glass. I strolled along my store's shelves of antique cookware, wineglass in hand. My store had been open for less than a year and it felt like I'd always been here. I guess that's a sign of being where you should be. I idly straightened a vintage grater here, an antique mixing bowl there, and blew a speck of dust off the heavy cast-iron meat grinder nobody ever bought. I didn't care. I loved the look and feel of it, a hand-cranked machine built to last. I loved the smell of my store, too. While meals were underway, it filled with the aromas of bacon, biscuits, and burgers. But at times like this, when it was just me and the store, I could inhale the seasoned scent of old wood and more than a century of memories.

At a plaintive mew from my apartment, I set the glass down. As soon as I opened the door, my foundling kitty Birdy streaked past into the restaurant. Like the wine, my tuxedo cat technically wasn't allowed in here, but the outer door was locked and I never let him stroll, wash, or catnap on any cooking surfaces.

"Was I ignoring you, little Birdman?" Always a streaker, he'd paused long enough to urgently lick a spot near his tail, so I had a moment to stroke his head. I knew I'd left him plenty of dry food and water when we'd gone out to Beanblossom. He hadn't been crying because he was hungry. He simply held a firm conviction everything was always more interesting on the other side of the door—any door.

I glanced at the clock and sighed. Nearly seven. In a scant twelve hours this place was going to be packed with hungry musicians and bluegrass fans, as well as the usual crew of locals. I'd better get some breakfast prep underway.

As I cut butter into flour for biscuits, as I measured out the dry ingredients for whole-wheat pancakes, as I cubed the green and orange flesh of ripe melons, my thoughts strayed to Pia Bianchi. She had quite the talent for getting people mad at her. I'd seen her in action at puzzle group, and she apparently wasn't paying her loan back to Sue. And to top it off with raising Abe's dander? She'd often seemed kind of defensive in the short time I'd known her, self-centered, too.

Maybe tomorrow I'd get a chance to ask Maria or Roberto what they knew about the reason for Pia coming to America and never going home. I thought most identical twins remained close their entire lives. Given how prickly Pia seemed, she could have had had a falling-out with her twin sister.

Chapter Four

As I'd expected, when I unlocked the front door at seven the next morning, the porch of my store was full of folks wanting breakfast. I welcomed them. My helper, Danna Beedle, and I were ready. Sausages sizzled and the pancake batter was mixed and ready to go. Two dozen biscuits waited hot and ready in the warmer. Our morning special was fried mush, always a favorite. Danna had arrived even before her usual time of six-thirty, saying she was ready for some action. Her cheeks were extra pink, which probably meant she'd spent the night with Isaac Rowling, her boyfriend who lived off the grid out in the woods. Danna had turned twenty recently, and even though she lived with her mother, the mayor of South Lick, Corrine didn't mind if Danna had slumber parties with Isaac.

"Good morning," I greeted the first couple, early morning regulars, and the dozen or so who followed them in. "Sit anywhere you can find a place." I hurried around pouring coffee and taking orders.

I smiled to see Adele and her steady guy Samuel grab the last open table.

I caught her gaze and held up a finger, indicating I'd get there as soon as I could. And I did, when things calmed down a little. I planted a kiss on her papery cheek and did the same for Samuel. Seventy-one and eighty-something, respectively, these seniors were marvels of energy and activity. Adele's cheeks were suspiciously pink, too. They'd probably come straight from their own sleepover. I approved, happy Adele had found love in her later years.

"What are you hungry for this morning?" I asked.

"Boy howdy, it smells good in here." Adele tilted her head back and inhaled deeply through her nose, smiling as she exhaled. "I'll have me some of that fried mush and an order of pancakes. What about you, honeyboo?" She patted Samuel's hand.

Samuel beamed at her. "The same, plus two fried eggs over easy, if you don't mind, Robbie. I got a hunger this morning."

I didn't ask him why. "Have you made it over to Beanblossom yet?"

"No, but we're planning to go today," Adele said. "The Good Ol' Persons are playing and I've been wanting to see them gals in person for a long time."

"It's an all-ladies bluegrass group from out your way," Samuel added. "San Francisco, if I'm not mistaken."

"I'd love to hear them," I said as Danna dinged the bell indicating an order was ready. "Right now I'd better get to work, though."

The next hour was consumed with one of the busiest breakfast days we'd had in quite a while.

The room buzzed with conversation punctuated by laughter, the clink of flatware on thick white plates, the sizzle of sausages atop the grill. Luckily Turner Rao, my other assistant cook—plus order taker, busboy, and dishwasher—showed up promptly at eight. The three of us did a well-choreographed dance until the rush lightened a few minutes before nine, when Roberto and Maria drifted downstairs, yawning. I hadn't heard them come in last night, having hit the sack before ten.

I greeted the pair and sat them at a table for two, glad the rush had let up a bit. I hadn't seen Chase or the other two guests yet. I opened my mouth to ask my father how the evening had gone when Buck ambled in through the door. Lieutenant Buck Bird, second in command in the South Lick police force. He was tall and skinny and possessed a truly hollow leg, eating more than I ever believed possible. Unlike most mornings, he didn't look either hungry or happy to be here.

He beckoned to me. I nodded my reply, then glanced around and gestured for Turner to come to Roberto and Maria's table. I introduced my assistant. "Turner will take your breakfast order, okay? I have to talk to the man who just came in."

That the man who just came in was Buck finally registered on Turner, whose pale brown skin suddenly lost its color.

"It's not about you, dude. You're fine," I whispered to Turner. He'd had a far too close encounter with murder this spring and I was sure the mere thought of a uniform made him blanch.

He swallowed. "Okay. Thanks, Robbie." He mustered a smile for the Italians.

When I reached Buck, I said, "What's up? You don't look your usual cheery self." Several murders had intersected my life over the last year. Buck had gotten used to accepting any information I happened to pick up about the crimes and the various persons of interest, as he put it. "Did something bad happen? Has there been another—"

"Keep your voice down now, Robbie," he said, cutting me off. He led me into the shelves of cookware. "How did you know we've had a homicide?" He bent his head down to peer at me, being over a foot taller than my five-foot-three.

"I didn't. You had that look on your face, plus you didn't come in wanting breakfast."

"I want breakfast, all right, or a second breakfast, to put it more accurately. But I got me a bigger mess than the *Deepwater Horizon* oil spill to deal with right now. You are correct. There was a suspicious death discovered this morning."

Another murder. "Who was it, and where?"

"An eyetalian lady. One Pia Bianchi," which he pronounced PYE-uh bye-ANCH-chee.

I sucked in a breath and brought my hand to my mouth. "Pia?" I whispered. *Oh, no.*

"Yeah. You knowed her?"

"I did. Not well. We were in a puzzle group together."

"When's last time you seen her?"

"Late yesterday afternoon at the music festival. She was playing with Abe O'Neill's bluegrass group."

Buck nodded slowly as if recording my words. "Time?" He pulled out a small notebook and a chewed-on pen and jotted down what I'd said.

"They stopped playing at five-thirty, five forty-five. We left and came home."

"Who's 'we'?"

"My father and his wife. They're visiting from Italy. I want you to meet them." I gazed in the direction of the restaurant portion of the store and took a step until Buck cleared his throat.

"Not right now, Robbie. I got a couple few more questions for you."

"But . . . why are you asking questions and not the state police detective?" Homicides in small Indiana towns were investigated by the state police, who worked with a Brown County crime task force. When the murder was local, town officers got involved and helped out with interviews and information gathering. Oscar Thompson had been the detective on the last murder in South Lick, and I hadn't found him either approachable or all that competent.

"Beanblossom's unincorporated, so it's county territory. Sheriff's department's handling the investigation, and they were kind enough"—Buck's mouth took a turn toward the sardonic—"to ask us local yokel police to help out. So just lemme ask the questions, all right? You happen to know of anybody who had a beef with Ms. Bianchi, any kind of a set-to? Witness any brouhahas involving her?"

Yikes. Had I ever. I swallowed. "Sue Berry—you know her, right?"

At his nod I went on. "She was upset with Pia last night. Said she'd lent her a lot of money and Pia wasn't paying it back. Sue's running the festival logistics this year. She'll be there all week."

"Duly noted."

"Then onstage Pia and Abe had a little argument. I'm sure it was nothing serious." Abe would never ever murder someone. I knew that as well as I knew my own heart. "The mikes were live, though, and everybody there heard it."

"Nothing else?"

"Well, Pia was a little prickly in our puzzle group. But not so much anybody would kill her for it." The poor woman. Her life cut short. I'd found her hard to get to know, hard to deal with, but that didn't mean I wanted her dead.

"Every scrap of information is part of the puzzle," Buck said. "You should oughta know that by now."

"Oh, and yesterday Beth Ferguson, one of my B&B guests, voiced a pretty extreme dislike for Pia. Not to me directly, but I overheard her and her boyfriend talking."

"She still here?" He jotted down the name.

"I haven't see her or Ed come down yet today, but they could have left by the upstairs exit."

"Boyfriend's name?"

"Ed Molina."

"Got it." Buck put away his notebook and stuck the pen above his ear. "Much obliged, Robbie."

"Wait," I said. "Was her body found in South Lick? Is that why you're on the case?"

He shook his head with a baleful air. "Fella by the name of Isaac Rowling found the body early this morning while out walking his dog. Did the right thing and called it in."

"Isaac?" *Danna's boyfriend.*

"I hear tell he's been dating Danna."

"He has. Where did he find Pia?"

Buck stared at me for a moment as if deciding whether to answer me or not. Finally he spoke. "Inside the Beanblossom covered bridge."

Chapter Five

Buck had already known Danna and Isaac were seeing each other, and he had the grace to ask me if I could spare her for a tiny small minute, as he put it, so he could confirm Isaac's story about where he'd been when the murder likely took place. I wondered if this meant the police knew of a connection between Pia and Isaac. I thought the person who reported the homicide was often automatically regarded as someone to investigate. The idea of finding a body in the covered bridge—the very bridge we'd driven through yesterday—made me feel sick. That and the stab of sadness at any violent death. Sadness tinged with fear if I was honest with myself, but I was too busy to dwell on any of those emotions. That would come later.

While Buck sat at the farthest table and questioned Danna about Isaac, I asked Turner to take over at the grill. I could wait tables and still catch up with my father and Maria. I supposed she was technically my stepmother, but since I'd never lived with her, the term seemed an odd one to use.

"Their order is ready," Turner said, gesturing to the plates.

"Thanks." I loaded a tray with a plate of biscuits and gravy, two eggs sunny-side up with hash browns, a stack of banana-walnut pancakes, and a serving of fried mush, and carried it to their table. The Italians were going all-American today.

"Did you hear some good tunes last night?" I asked after I distributed the plates where they belonged. I smiled at Maria and attempted some halting Italian for her benefit. "*Ti piace la musica?*"

"*Sì, mi è piaciuto molto.*" She smiled back and nodded.

"*Bene,*" I said. Good.

"We saw Mr. Broward play," Roberto said. "He is very good. I wanted to speak with Pia, but we only saw her far away and then she left."

Pia. Now the late Pia. Buck might want to speak with Roberto next. I glanced around the room. The diners at the few other occupied tables were all busy eating and talking, or in the case of two of my regulars, playing chess at the table where I'd painted a chessboard on the surface. I pulled up a chair and sat.

"That man who came in?"

"*La polizia?*"

Right. Buck was in uniform. I barely even noticed anymore. "Yes. I'm afraid Pia died."

Maria's brow knit. "Died? *Morto?*"

I nodded. "Worse. I'm sorry to say she was killed. Murdered." I wasn't going to tell them she was found in the bridge. Let them keep a happy memory of yesterday, not a horrific one.

Maria gasped and crossed herself. Roberto's expression turned somber.

"This is terrible. But this police, he thinks you are involved?" my father asked, peering into my face.

"No. None of us here. But the young man who found her is Danna's boyfriend, so Buck needed to ask her some questions. If you don't mind, I'll tell him you saw her at the festival last night. And that you realized you know her family. It might be important."

Roberto nodded, but stole a glance at Maria as if unsure she would agree.

The cowbell on the door jangled and my friend Philostrate MacDonald pushed through it with his back. His arms held two trays of brownies. "Bet you thought I forgot, right Robbie?" he called to me.

"I wasn't worried," I responded. Phil was my very reliable baker as well as my friend. "Set those down and come meet some people."

He shook my father's hand as I introduced everybody. Phil smiled at Maria, too.

"I'm really glad to meet you both," he said. "You can't believe how excited Robbie was to find you last fall, Mr. Fracasso."

"And I, her, right, *cara mia*?" Roberto said, patting his wife's hand. She nodded with a smile for me.

"Phil is Samuel's grandson, and he also bakes my lunch desserts," I told them. "Delicious brownies and more."

Phil's dark skin glowed. "I had a super idea. I picked up some vanilla ice cream on the way over.

I'll make brownie ice cream sandwiches for you to
serve as a lunch special. What do you think?"

Yum. "I love it," I said. "You're brilliant."

"Great. Lemme get the ice cream out of my car."
He surveyed the room. "Uh-oh. Why is Buck talking
with Danna? She's not in trouble, is she?"

"No. But her boyfriend Isaac had the misfortune
to find the body of a murder victim this morning.
I'm sure Buck is only confirming his story."

A door slammed upstairs and footsteps heralded
Chase appearing at the bottom of the staircase over on
the other side of the store. I waved a hand, then focused on my friend again, whose back was to Chase.

"I heard the end of a news flash concerning it on
my way over, but I didn't realize you were involved."
Phil whistled. "Another murder, Robbie," he murmured.

"I'm afraid so. At least I'm not involved . . . for a
change."

"Who was the poor guy?" Phil asked.

"It was a woman. Her name is, or was, Pia Bianchi.
We saw her play at the music festival yesterday."

Phil's startling blue eyes widened. "Pia? Our Pia?"

I cocked my head. "What do you mean, our Pia?"

"She's a music student at IU. You know, in my department. She's a really nice lady." His eyes filled.

"I didn't know." At least somebody had liked Pia. I
shook my head. I checked for Chase, but he'd disappeared. He was probably browsing the cookware,
as he'd said, to pick up something for his wife. "I
wonder if Buck knows she was a student. I didn't, but
we'd only seen each other a couple times."

Phil blinked away a tear, swiping at the corners of

his eyes. "It's super sad she was killed," he said, his usual exuberant spirits dimmed a notch. "I'd better take a number and get in line to tell Buck what I know. But first, ice cream."

"Turner can help you assemble the sandwiches," I said. "They should freeze for a couple hours before the lunch crowd, right?"

Phil nodded and pivoted toward the door.

"What did he mean by another murder?" my father asked.

I grimaced. I hadn't filled Roberto in on that particular aspect of my life, not in e-mails, nor when I'd visited him in Italy over New Year's. "We have had a bit of bad luck since last fall. Three different people were killed around here, two in South Lick. I found one of the bodies right here in my store, and once my friend and I happened across another one. I feel a little jinxed."

"What is jinxed?" Roberto asked.

"It means prone to bad luck."

"*Sfortuna*," Maria whispered.

I dipped my head once. "Exactly."

Chapter Six

Twenty minutes later Roberto sat across the table from Buck. Maria had gone back up to the room. Phil and Turner were busy cutting brownies and spreading softened ice cream on squares, and Danna was on the grill. Meanwhile I delivered a Kitchen Sink omelet with hash browns and fried mush to Chase Broward. He was the only diner in the place at the moment and sat at a small table near the door with his back to the rest of the restaurant. His guitar case rested on the floor next to him.

"My parents said they enjoyed your playing last night."

"Glad to hear it." He beamed his smooth smile at me. "I trust they got home safely."

"Yes, they did, thanks. Since it's light until quite a bit after nine, they didn't have a problem."

Chase took a sip of coffee. "I was reading the news online upstairs. There was a short piece saying a body was found in Beanblossom. The article said it was being treated as a suspicious death. I hope they don't cancel the festival because of it."

"I hadn't thought of that." I'd been thinking of poor Pia, not about the festival. It seemed like a cold reaction from him. But I supposed if he hadn't known Pia, and if he had a passion for bluegrass music . . . Still, for a glad-hander like him thinking of running for national office, showing a bit more empathy might have been in order.

"Did you know Pia Bianchi?" I asked him. "She was onstage earlier yesterday."

He blinked and glanced past me toward the door. "No, never met her."

"Well, enjoy your breakfast. Are you playing tonight, too?"

Chase nodded, mouth now full of eggs, gaze already on the urgent business of his phone.

I moseyed over to the grill. My tall and ever-stylish assistant today wore a lilac bandanna over her red-gold dreadlocks, and a pink T-shirt under purple striped overalls. Pink high-tops finished the outfit. I'd told her early on that as long as her clothes were clean and her hair covered, I didn't care what she wore. Me? I saved style for after hours, dressing for work nearly every day in jeans and a store T-shirt. Short sleeves in the warmer weather, long sleeves when it was cold. I pinned the curly black hair I'd gotten from Roberto back with a strong clip and usually didn't even wear earrings to work.

"Danna, how did it go with Buck?"

She scrubbed the grill a little harder than she needed to. "He didn't seem to believe me that I was with Isaac all night until I left at six to get here on time. I told him twenty times it was true, and that

Isaac was heading out to jog with the dog. He goes early every day, before he leaves for work."

"Does he live close to Beanblossom?"

"Yeah, maybe a mile from the bridge. It's part of his route because the bridge road is so small there's never any traffic." She wrinkled her nose. "Buck said Isaac called about the body from some minister's house. I have no idea why he didn't have his phone with him. Buck seemed to think that was suspicious behavior."

"Did Isaac know Pia?"

"I don't know. Buck asked me the same question. I never heard Isaac talk of her, but that doesn't mean he didn't know her."

I looked over when I saw Buck stand and shake Roberto's hand. "Maria went upstairs," I called to him. My father nodded and headed in the same direction. Buck strolled toward Danna and me. Danna twisted her mouth like she'd tasted a spoiled sausage and scrubbed even harder. Buck beckoned me away from the stove.

"Did you learn what you needed?" I asked him.

"Maybe. You know I got to tell the sheriff your papa knew the deceased."

I stared at him. "Why? He didn't kill Pia. He hadn't even seen her in twenty years or more."

"And I'm sure the sheriff's detective will decide he's exactly what he seems, a foreign visitor with no role in the murder. Still and all, I got to tell her." Buck lowered his voice. "Who's the customer?"

I also spoke softly. "His name is Chase Broward. He's a B&B guest and a musician, but he's also a city councillor in Bloomington. He said he's thinking of running for Senate, though."

"Thought he looked familiar. So he was at the festival yesterday?"

"He played last night. I asked him a few minutes ago if he knew Pia and he said he didn't."

"Doing my job for me, Robbie?"

I shook my head. "No, of course not. He said he'd read online that the body had been found."

"So the news is out. Great." Buck's voice belied his words. "I guess we can't expect it to be a secret."

"But Phil knows Pia." I gestured with my chin toward the dessert assembly line a few yards away. "Phil, can you talk to Buck while you're wrapping desserts?"

"Sure," Phil replied.

I looked at Danna. "Take your break while it's quiet, okay?"

"Thanks." She slid off her apron and strode for the restroom.

I realized I should have offered earlier. "Turner, take yours as soon as you're done with the ice cream sandwiches."

"Yes, boss." He gave me a brownie-coated thumbs-up, his color and equilibrium clearly restored.

"Morning, Buck," Phil said. "I'm in the same department at IU as Pia. Or I was, I suppose. It's terrible news."

"Every homicide is," Buck replied. "That said, I'm here gathering facts from the locals, as the sheriff's detective put it." He wrinkled his nose. "Phil, when's the last time you seen Ms. Bianchi?" He murdered the pronunciation again and I cringed.

Phil glanced over at me, trying to keep a grin off his face. "Today's Wednesday. So it must have been Monday in Bloomington. We both had a rehearsal for *Aida.* That lady could sing like nobody's business."

"And for Italian operas, she already knew the language," I said.

"Exactly," Phil agreed.

"So Monday. What time would you say?" Buck chewed on the end of his pen.

If Adele were here she'd warn him the end of that pen would come off one of these days and he'd have a mouthful of ink. And he'd probably ignore her.

"Six p.m. or so, I'd say. Rehearsal went long." Phil checked the clock, which read 11:00. "I'd better go. I have to be at work at noon." He enclosed the last sandwich in plastic wrap and handed Turner the tray of neatly wrapped brown and white square desserts. "Into the Deepfreeze with these."

"Yes, sir," Turner said.

"Thank you, Phil," I called as he passed Chase's table.

Phil turned, his hand rising to acknowledge my thanks. He looked at Chase's face and froze. He shifted his gaze, staring at Buck and me, then walked briskly back toward us. "That guy," he whispered.

Buck frowned. "What about him?"

Phil's nostrils flared. "He was having an affair with Pia."

Chapter Seven

After assuring Buck he wasn't mistaken, Phil made his exit out the service door.

To avoid Chase seeing him, I supposed. So Chase lied to me about knowing Pia. If he was married, and it was an illicit affair, that could easily be the reason for the untruth.

It didn't take long for Buck to approach Chase. I moseyed nearby and began to wipe down empty tables. The lunch rush would be upon us before long.

"Excuse me, sir," Buck said. "I'm Lieutenant Bird of the South Lick police."

"Chase Broward, sir." He jumped to his feet and pumped Buck's hand. "Thank you for your service, Lieutenant. I'm glad to make your acquaintance."

Buck extracted his hand. "You may have heard we had a suspicious death here in the county, Mr. Broward."

Chase adopted a sincere expression. "Yes, I did. It's a sad day, may she rest in peace." He clasped his hands in front of his waist. When he darted his gaze to me and back to Buck, his expression was more annoyed than sincere.

"So you know it was a female." Buck had an aw-shucks manner about him, with a relaxed, twangy speech to match, but if there was anything I'd learned in the last year it was that his hillbilly manner masked a truly sharp intellect and years of experience on the force. There were no flies on Buck Bird, as Adele would say—and had.

"Did you happen to learn the name of the deceased?" Buck continued.

Chase frowned and gazed at the corner of the room. "I can't quite recall."

Well, that was horseradish. I'd told him Pia's name myself. Could Chase truly have forgotten something from half an hour ago? I finished cleaning all the tables within earshot and hurried off to grab fresh paper place mats and the silverware we rolled in blue cloth napkins. When I came back, my guest had crossed his arms over his chest.

"I dunno," Buck said. "We got us a witness says you were stepping out with Ms. Bianchi, so to speak."

A flash of brilliance struck me. "Buck, I don't want to intrude, but I snapped a photo of Pia onstage last night. Do you want to see?" I'd zoomed in and taken a couple yesterday as Abe's group was playing. In one number Pia had played right next to my boyfriend, so she had to be in the shot, too. I hadn't had time to crop or otherwise process the photographs.

Buck barely restrained himself from rolling his eyes, but restrain he did. "Why, that might could be right useful, Robbie."

I dug my phone out of my back pocket and swiped

through the pictures from last night until I found the best one of Pia. Abe was making an odd expression, so it definitely wasn't the best of him.

"Here." I extended the phone to Buck, who indicated I should go ahead and show Chase.

He bent his silver head and studied the photo, then straightened, handing the phone back to me. "I know the woman," he said to Buck. "But she told me her name was Patricia. Patty White." He smiled without much enthusiasm. "That's why I said I didn't know her."

Bianchi meant *white* in English. Either she had been disguising her identity—or he knew some Italian and was lying. Before my few experiences with murderers over the last year, I'd been a lot more willing to give people the benefit of the doubt and trust their word. Of course, all kinds of people lie for all kinds of reasons. It comes with the territory when a man or a woman has taken another's life and is desperate to avoid being accused of the deadly crime.

I pocketed my phone and resumed setting up tables. I eavesdropped through the next few more minutes of Buck talking with Chase. The main things said were yes, Chase had known Pia, and no, he hadn't killed her.

"You're a married man, ain't you, Mr. Broward?" Buck asked. "Didja maybe know Ms. Bianchi in the Biblical sense?"

Chase's nostrils flared ever so slightly. "I can't see what business it is of yours, Lieutenant."

"When we're investigating a murder, everything is our business."

"I made the mistake of getting carried away with

Ms. White one night. That's all it was." He lifted his chin.

By now I wasn't even pretending not to listen.

Buck scribbled in his notebook. Without looking up, he asked, "How long were you in Beanblossom yesterday, and when did you arrive back here?"

Chase cleared his throat. "I was onstage at the festival until ten o'clock and then drove back. Alone."

I made a mental note to ask Roberto if he'd heard Chase come in and if he'd noted the time.

Buck jotted down Chase's cell number and address and thanked him. "We'd appreciate you not leaving town until further notice."

Chase raised his eyebrows. "Lieutenant, I'd planned to be here through Sunday. But I live a scant thirty miles to the west. Surely you can find me if you need me."

"All right. But don't be traveling outside the state, or heck, even north of Martinsville. Do I have your word?"

"Very well."

Buck nodded.

Chase in turn thanked me, although I expected he was probably cursing me silently at the same time. "I won't be back until late tonight," he told me. "Jam sessions all afternoon."

"Enjoy." I watched him carry out the guitar case, letting the screen door slam behind him.

"Whooee," Buck said, scratching his head so his thin hair stuck up like the fur on a spooked cat. "I'm so hungry my belly thinks my throat's been cut."

I winced. "Buck!"

"Guess that's not a particularly appropriate thing

to say today, is it? Anyhoo, I been up since before the rooster put his pants on. Any chance of an early lunch?"

"Of course. The usual?"

He was already pulling out a chair at a small table. "Whatever you got. But tell me one thing. Did you hear this Broward character come in last night or go out sometime before dawn?"

I shook my head. "I'm afraid I didn't hear a thing. My guests get a key to their separate entrance. It and their parking area are on the other side of the building from my apartment. Plus I wear earplugs when I sleep. Sorry."

"Maybe your other guests heard him." He sat and extracted his phone from his shirt pocket.

To relay the new information to headquarters, I imagined.

"Hey, Robbie?" Danna called.

I made my way to the cooking area where Turner had finished cleaning up after the ice cream and brownie effort. He sat at a table making his way through a big plate of brunch.

"Can you order in some soba noodles if you can get them, or vermicelli if you can't?" he asked. "In Bloomington last week, I had an Asian noodle salad to die for. I re-created it at home, and I think our customers will love it."

"Got it." I thumbed a quick reminder to myself on my phone. I threw two meat patties on the clean grill for Buck, popped open halves of a bun in the toaster, and scooped out potato salad into a small bowl. "That was quite a morning," I said to Danna. "Have you talked with Isaac yet?"

"He's supposed to be working at the state park, but I put in a call to him, anyway," she answered, pulling open the heavy walk-in cooler door. "He hasn't called back. I hope he's not getting grilled by that weird detective dude." She disappeared inside.

She must mean Oscar Thompson, the detective on the most recent murder. No, Buck had referred to the detective as a female. I flipped his meat patties, the smell of which were making me super hungry. I topped both with cheddar cheese and had set up a plate with the requisite pickle spear, lettuce, and tomato when my cell rang. I glanced at Turner and pointed to the burgers, but the young man was already on his feet and heading to the stove to finish Buck's order.

I walked to the open front door to answer the call, slipping out the screen door as I heard Abe's sexy baritone on the line.

"Robbie, I heard the news about Pia." He sounded worried.

"I did, too. It's been, shall we say, an interesting morning around here. You're at work, right?"

"Yes, but I'm ready to take my lunch break. I thought I'd drop by for a burger, but what I really want is to talk with you."

"I know. Me, too. Let me see what Roberto and Maria are up to for the rest of the day. I'll know by the time you get here."

"That's unlikely." The worry switched to laughter as he pulled his truck into one of the diagonal spaces right in front of me. He waved through the open window.

A smile split my face. I loved this guy. Before he could even open his door, though, another call came in. I disconnected his and answered Sue Berry's call.

"Robbie, I need your help." Her voice was low, urgent.

"What's happened, Sue? Are you okay? The family, the baby?" Her first granddaughter had been born only six months ago.

"They're all fine. It's me."

"What's the matter? Where are you?"

"At the Nashville sheriff's station." Her voice rose to a near screech. "They think I killed Pia!"

Chapter Eight

I sat in a rocker on the porch and managed to talk Sue down off the cliff. She was too frazzled to give me many details, and it turned out she hadn't been arrested for the crime, merely asked to come to the station to be questioned.

"But I can't get hold of my husband, Robbie. I need Glen to call our lawyer." Her tone was still frantic, but slightly less panicked.

"I'll do my best to find him." Glen Berry was the owner of a successful small liquor store chain in the area. "You just sit tight, okay? I'll get through to him."

"But what about the festival? What if it falls apart because I'm not there?" she wailed.

"Sue, it's going to be fine. You've set everything up to run smoothly, and I'm positive it will." I had no idea if that was true, but what else could I say? "I'll check in with you later."

"Thank you, Robbie. You're the good friend I need right now." She said good-bye and disconnected.

I stared at my phone. Sue must have accosted Pia in public about the debt again last night and someone reported it. But the detective would need evidence to actually arrest her.

"Earth to Robbie," Abe said from the top step, waving one of the purple-checked handkerchiefs he always carried.

I looked up into his concerned face. "I'm sorry. Sue is at the county sheriff's station in Nashville. They're asking her questions about Pia, and she can't find her husband. Glen apparently is the only one who knows who their lawyer is."

Abe sank into the rocker next to me and laid his hand on my knee. "She's not the only one they want to talk to. I got a call, too. Apparently my amplified argument with Pia didn't go unnoticed." He wore the rural electric company summer uniform of a green polo shirt with their logo on the pocket and darker green work pants.

"Ouch."

"It won't be a problem. I didn't see her again after our last number. I left, picked up Sean at math club, and spent the evening with him."

"How's he doing?" I asked.

"Good. Thirteen going on twenty, of course. Looking forward to spending most of the summer with my folks, mostly because Dad will probably teach him to drive on the back roads." Abe shook his head, his dimple deepening. "I keep telling my boy that thirteen is not sixteen, but he doesn't seem to get the message."

My mind couldn't seem to leave Pia's murder.

"Did he stay overnight?" I asked. Abe was going to need an airtight alibi.

"No. He'd forgotten to bring a school library book that was due today, so I took him back to his mom's." Abe gazed at me. "I didn't go find Pia and kill her on my way home. Don't worry."

"Of course you didn't. But you're going to have to convince the detective of that." I gazed across the street at the woods in full leaf and varying shades of green. Someone had mowed a lawn nearby, and a small plane droned overhead. On such a sunny day, the warm air made me want to drop everything and ride my bike to a lake for the rest of the day. Too bad that wasn't going to happen.

"Why would I murder someone because she wanted to mess up our festival gig?"

I raised a shoulder and let it drop, focusing on Abe again. "Pia wasn't a regular member of your bluegrass group, was she? I don't remember seeing her the last time you guys played."

"No. Bud wanted to bring her in for a trial. She'd only rehearsed with us twice. She had a great voice and was a decent banjo player, but I think she thought she would become the star. It was a little early for that."

"Phil said she's a fellow music student with him at IU. That she sang opera, too."

Abe let out a breath. "Not anymore, sadly."

My stomach growled.

Abe laughed the deep rolling laugh I adored. "Sounds like we're both hungry." He stood and held out a hand. "Can I take you to lunch?"

I let him help me up. "Only if you let me cook it."

Buck pushed out through the doorway at the same time two carloads of diners pulled up. "Morning, O'Neill." He bit into the ice cream sandwich in his hand.

Abe returned the greeting.

Buck swallowed and went on. "You're on my list of folks to track down, but I got me a call from headquarters. Been called to a meeting, some kind of powwow. Be seeing you down there later, I expect." He tipped his hat. "Great lunch, Robbie. Simple and filling, exactly how I like it."

"See you, Buck." I frowned as he went. Abe not having an alibi worried me. A lot.

Chapter Nine

I ran my tail off for the next hour and a half. The two carloads of hungry music festival folks had swarmed in and were only the beginning of a major lunch rush. Thank goodness for Danna and Turner, and I was glad I'd gotten in a quick chat with Abe while I could. He'd eaten a quick grilled ham and cheese sandwich and had taken a brownie ice cream sandwich to go, promising to call me later.

One customer I hadn't seen in a while was Paula Berry, Sue and Glen's daughter. She'd come in a little bit ago with another woman around her age, each pushing a stroller. I grimaced inwardly. Did she know of her mother's predicament? I took over the sodas they'd ordered from Danna and resolved not to bring up Sue's current location unless Paula did.

I greeted her and asked, "How's that baby?" I peered in to see the fat-cheeked little girl sucking her toe and burbling in baby dialect.

"Susannah is doing so well. She's six months old tomorrow."

"She looks healthy and happy. What else could

you want?" Besides a father to help raise her, but that
was a different issue. What was done was done.

"She really is." Paula introduced me to her friend,
who had a baby boy the same size as little Susannah.
He looked like he was ready to go to sleep.

"Nice to meet you," I said. "Paula, I saw your mom
at the music festival last night. Sue's doing a great job
managing it."

"I know. She absolutely loves it. Heck, she's managed our family all these years. She's simply taking it
to another level." She wrinkled her nose. "Too bad
my father doesn't think so."

"Oh?" I asked.

"Dad is such a dinosaur. He doesn't want her to
have a job. It's so stupid. I mean, I love her having
lots of time to babysit. But there's more to life than
only taking care of other people, well, unless it's your
job." She shook her head. "Mom likes running things
and she's good at it. He shouldn't get so upset that
she's out doing something she loves."

Her friend nodded in agreement.

"He's probably used to the status quo," I said.
"Don't you think he'll come around?"

"Maybe. I don't know. They've been squabbling a
lot more lately. Just kind of picking at each other."

"Every relationship goes through its rough spots."
I heard the ding of the food-ready bell. "Let me go
get your orders."

"One second. Robbie," Paula beckoned me closer.
"Did you hear a woman was killed?" she whispered.

I nodded. "It's a sad day in the county."

Paula shuddered. "All I can picture is Erica." Her

eyes filled. It had been Paula's sister Erica's body I'd found in my store last November.

Her friend reached over and rubbed Paula's shoulder, even while keeping her baby's stroller gently moving back and forth with her foot.

Paula smiled wanly and took a sip of her soda. "I'm okay."

I patted her other shoulder. At least she didn't seem to know about her mom being questioned. She would later, but she might as well enjoy her lunch while she could.

At twelve-forty, Roberto and Maria came downstairs, she with a purse hanging from the crook of her elbow, both carrying light jackets. I hurried over to greet them.

"We're going to visit Bloomington for the rest of the day. You're busy and"—Roberto's arm tightened around his wife's shoulders—"Maria, she is a little upset by all the talk of murder."

Maria nodded slowly. "I sorry, Roberta," she murmured.

Now that I took a good look at her, she did look a bit pale, with new lines around her eyes.

"That's fine," I said. "Go. There's so much to see and do in Bloomington."

"Yes," agreed Roberto. "And I want to show her where I studied all those years ago."

All those years ago when he and my mom fell in love. When they conceived me. When he had the quarry accident that ended his graduate fellowship. He'd returned to Italy before Mom knew she was pregnant. For reasons I never knew, she didn't tell him, didn't write him a letter, didn't search him out.

She left her sister Adele and moved to Santa Barbara. I hadn't missed having a father, really, because she and I were so happy as a mother-daughter unit—until she died suddenly, way too young, a year and a half ago. I was already working as a chef here in southern Indiana, so I let Adele comfort me, and ended up buying and renovating my country store. But it wasn't until last fall that I solved the puzzle of who my father had been.

"Enjoy yourselves." I meant it. They didn't need to stay here among the craziness that was a too-full restaurant and a murder investigation, to boot. I embraced Maria and came away with the lovely scent of her perfume in my nose.

"We'll stay out for dinner, too," he added.

"Sounds good." I gave him a hug, too. Off they went, and back I went to busing tables, making change, taking orders, and generally filling in wherever Danna and Turner needed me.

During a temporary lull, when everyone was served and no tables needed clearing and setting up, I should have finally grabbed a bite to eat. Instead, I dashed to my desk in the corner and looked up the numbers for all five of Glen Berry's liquor stores. I should have gotten his cell number from Sue. Too late for that now. I didn't reach him until my fourth call.

"Glen, it's Robbie Jordan."

"Robbie, nice to talk to you. What can I help you with?"

"Did you speak with Sue yet?" I waited while he gave instructions to someone in the background.

"Sorry about that." His voice lowered. "I got her message, and the lawyer should oughta be there by now. I told her not to lend that woman money, but she wasn't having it. Pia Bianchi was another way to spell trouble, no mistake about it."

"Why did Pia need money? And how did Sue know her?"

"For corn sake, Pia wanted to go be an opera singer. Costs an arm and a leg to take classes over there at the U. Pia could have been satisfied with singing in the church choir like Sue was. No, that Italian was your common slut who thought she was better than she ever would be. And that's all I'll say on the subject."

Ouch. Tell me how you really feel, Glen.

"So Sue met her at church?"

"Yep. Brought her home for dinner one time, then had the nerve to ask me to drive the lady home."

"Were you at the festival last night, too?"

"Me?" he scoffed. "Can't stand that kind of music. Give me a good mellow jazz, not plucking and fiddling. Just plain hurts my ears. No, I was right here at home, but Susie was there real late."

Uh-oh. Another lack of alibi. Unless Pia had been killed early enough in the evening Sue would still have been at the festival. I didn't envy the detective on the case.

"Don't know why she took on the dang fool job, anyways," Glen went on. "We got plenty of money. I make enough for both of us. She used to be happy taking care of the kids and the house and whatnot."

I could almost hear him roll his eyes. I rolled mine, too, because he'd confirmed what Paula had said. Talk about a dinosaur. What century was he living in, anyway?

Danna dinged the food-ready bell twice, and Turner cast me a frantic look. "I have to get back to work, Glen. Sue asked me to help find you, so I'm glad you got connected."

"All righty then, Robbie. You have a good day, now."

All righty. He didn't much like Pia, that was clear. One of the only things that was clear right now.

Chapter Ten

At two-twenty, Ed and Beth clattered down the stairs. It was quiet enough that I'd finally cooked up a turkey burger for myself and was in the process of inhaling it. Only one other couple occupied a table.

"Are we too late to eat?" she asked.

Tired though I was, I mustered a smile. "You made it down in time. Sit anywhere." I'd told my guests they could cash in the breakfast part of B&B during any of the hours I was open. These two were either serious night owls or had been having a lot of fun up there all day. At least I hadn't heard a thing, not a footstep nor a bed squeak. My soundproofing of the ceiling had been successful. I hadn't been sure it would be in such an old building.

"Thanks," Ed said. "Would you happen to still be serving breakfast?" The sides and back of his black hair were cut short, and the rest was pulled up in a man-bun like the fiddler's in Abe's group. A stupid term, really. It was simply a bun. On a man. His was wet, like he'd just gotten out of a shower, and he smelled like he'd used the little bottle of apple-scented shampoo I stocked in the bathrooms.

"You're welcome to anything on the breakfast menu, but we've run out of our special today, the fried mush," I said.

Danna had already erased the mush from the Specials blackboard and replaced it with Kahlua Brownie Ice Cream Sandwich.

"Not a problem," Ed assured me.

Beth was again wearing the kind of Depression-era outfit Danna sometimes did. Her worn cotton-print dress looked like it was Dust Bowl vintage, and her dark socks and heavy-soled leather shoes were no-nonsense, too.

"Your clogging was pretty amazing yesterday," I said with a smile.

She returned the smile. "Thanks. I love it."

"Have you been clogging long?"

"I've been doing some kind of dance my whole life. And when I saw cloggers, I knew I had to try it." Beth's face lit up. "It's cool to free-style. That's what we were doing last night. It's like you become another instrument and you start clogging rhythmically off what the other clogger and the other musicians are doing."

Ed spoke up. "Exactly. We're all jamming off each other."

"What's awesome is when you're driving home after a dance session," Beth continued. "Suddenly you hear a rhythm in your head and you start imagining new steps. It can make it very hard to go to bed at night."

"No kidding." Ed rolled his eyes, but in an affectionate way.

"Robbie, we'll be out until late again, so you can do up the room any time," Beth said.

I cleared my throat. "I'm sorry. We don't service the rooms unless you stay more than a week. It's posted in the room and on our Web site." I was a new innkeeper. Adele had suggested a policy of no room freshening when I'd been wondering how I could afford to hire someone to do it for me. With only three rooms, I could have managed, but I was interested in having a life, too. As it was, I still had to do the cleaning and laundry when rooms turned over. Half the time I was hard pressed just to get my ordering and restaurant prep done for the next day, so I hadn't been quite sure how to fit in B&B-necessary work, too. "It's one way I keep my costs down." And speaking of costs, I hoped they'd been telling Sue the truth yesterday and would pay up what they owed the festival today.

"That's fine," Ed said, nudging his partner/ girlfriend/wife, whatever she was.

"Sure," Beth said, although it didn't really seem fine, judging from the expression on her face.

I hailed Turner and asked him to take their order. After I finished my burger, I flipped the sign on the door to CLOSED at exactly two-thirty. I wasn't letting anybody else in today. We'd made a boatload of money and then some. Now was the time to clean and regroup.

"I was thinking to whip up some sugar cream pies for lunch tomorrow," Danna said when I returned to the kitchen area. "You good with that?"

Sugar cream pies? A signature dessert in these parts, one that made diners of almost any age think fondly of their grandmothers, and a pie a lot of restaurants no longer offered. "Of course. Great idea. But let me make them later today. It'll relax me to bake when it's quiet." After I squeezed in a bike ride, that is.

"You're the boss, boss." Danna grabbed a damp rag and started wiping down tables.

Turner handed me Beth and Ed's order. "Want me to cook?"

"I can do it. Can you start cleanup?"

"Sure." Turner immersed his arms in a sink full of soapy water. "I'll do the grill when you're done."

"Thanks," I checked the order slip, then slapped two patties on the grill, one veggie and one beef, and set up two plates. I scooted over to a two-top who looked like they'd finished. "Can I get you all anything else?"

"No, thank you. But everything was perfect." The woman had a whimsical floating musical staff on her T-shirt. "Them ice cream sandwiches were pure heaven on a plate."

"Glad you liked them. Looks like you're heading over to the festival." I fished their check out of my apron pocket and laid it facedown on the table before I picked up their plates.

"You bet," the man said, sporting a grinning fiddle on his own shirt. "We have jam sessions all afternoon today."

The woman raised her eyebrows. "Heared y'all had a murder around these parts." She made a tsking sound. "Do you think it's safe for us to go back to Beanblossom?"

"I'm sure it is," I replied. "The county sheriffs are excellent at their job." That is, I hoped they were. None of the murders I'd had the bad luck to be associated with had taken place in unincorporated areas, so the South Lick police had been assisted by state police detectives.

"Hon, I told you we'll be fine." The man winked at me. "We'll only be with a few thousand other musicians."

"Well, I ain't going into no covered bridge, I'll tell you that much." She stood. "They make me nervous even when some lady hasn't upped and got herself killed in one."

"I know what you mean. Thanks for coming in," I said. "I hope you'll come back."

"Say, you ever cook up some sugar cream pies?" the man asked with a hopeful look.

"Funny you asked. They're our special for tomorrow." I smiled. Now I was sure they'd be back.

Chapter Eleven

Two hours later I'd gotten out for a hard half-hour ride on my bike, and was back, showered, fed, and ready to bake. Riding the scenic hills of the county restored my equilibrium better than anything. Oxygen in, muscles stretched and worked, brain cleared. It did all of that, and more.

As I rolled out piecrust after piecrust, though, all the events of the day, all the conversations and theories about the murder flooded back into my mind. Glen expressing his dislike for Pia, and Beth doing the same. Sue's anger and frustration at not having her loan repaid. Chase saying he'd had a one-night stand with the victim, but Phil indicating it had been more than that. Even Roberto and Maria acknowledging they knew the Bianchi family back in Italy. Abe's lack of alibi. Heck, everybody's lack of alibi, as far as I could tell.

What was the county sheriff's detective going to do with the information Buck had gathered? Surely the department had a team out gathering even more. They had to be checking alibis at the very least. They were probably looking into Pia's movements and finances. A crime scene team must have searched the bridge and the surrounding area for evidence as to the murderer's identity. I wished I knew more. What time was she killed? Was she killed there or taken to the bridge? What time had Isaac found her? And did he have any association with Pia?

By now I'd filled ten pie pans. I pricked the crusts, laid a circle of parchment paper on each, weighted them down with the ceramic marbles I used as pie weights, then popped half of them into my super-wide preheated oven for a quick bake. The others I carried into the walk-in to stay cool. Now for the filling, a recipe I'd gotten from Jane Carter, a customer who was from around here but had moved out of state. She came in every time she returned to Indiana, though, to say hi, eat, and shop for more cookware, especially pie pans. I took a moment to try Sue's number, since I'd promised to check in with her. I reached only her voice-mail, so I left a quick message saying I was thinking of her.

I melted butter, sugar, and cornstarch in a saucepan, then added half-and-half, milk, vanilla, and salt. I turned down the temperature and stirred, waiting for the filling to thicken. I did some thinking, too. When the timer dinged, I pulled out the piecrusts and slid the others in.

Twenty minutes later all the crusts were filled, all the pies dusted with cinnamon on top. Was there anything more satisfying than seeing ten pies lined up cooling? Solving a crossword came close. Solving a murder did, too, but that was a dangerous job best left to the professionals, no matter how much my brain was suited to the work. I didn't have all the other training and wasn't really interested in signing up for it. How to shoot a gun, how to analyze fingerprints, how to safely take down someone who presented a threat, even how to use a Taser. My strengths lay elsewhere and I was the first to acknowledge it.

My mom had taught me that. I could still hear her voice echoing in my head. "Nobody's good at everything, honey," she'd said when I was a perfectionist fourteen-year-old bemoaning another girl besting me on debate team. "We each have our strengths. And I'm willing to bet that other girl doesn't know the first thing about beveling a corner or driving a straight nail." At that I'd smiled, because I'd been learning carpentry from Mom since I was little.

I sighed, missing her all over again. Her death from an aneurysm had been sudden, unexpected, and deeply unsettling, tossing my whole world into a tumble. She and I had been so close, and I'd thought she'd always be there for me.

But this—I gazed around my beloved store and restaurant, which I'd renovated using every skill Mom had taught me and then some—this business for which I had a passion was made possible in large part because of the money I inherited after her death. She'd taken good care of her finances, for her cabinetry business and her personal life. She'd had all her affairs in order when she died, despite being only in her fifties, an age when most healthy people don't expect to shuffle off this mortal coil.

My cell rang with Abe's ringtone. "Hey, sweet cheeks." I could hear the smile in my voice.

He growled. "I love it when you talk sugar to me. I'd prefer dirty, but a man takes what he's given."

I laughed. "What's up, Mr. O'Neill?"

"Just got done talking with the sheriff's detective. I think, and I qualify that with *think*, I convinced her I didn't have any past rancorous history with Pia and no way would I have killed her because of a silly—"

"But public," I interjected.

"But public, argument about a gig playlist."

"Lack of alibi notwithstanding."

"Yes. It's early days, no, early hours yet in their investigation, so I'm sure she could drum up something and ask me to come back in."

"The detective is a woman, then." Buck had said *she* or *her*, too, come to think of it.

"Yep. Anne Henderson. Seems competent, straightforward. All business."

"I hope she won't ask you back," I said.

"You and me both, Ms. Jordan. I called to see if you wanted to grab some dinner and head back to the festival tonight." He lowered his voice to a sexy husky timbre. "And I don't have my son tonight, so . . ."

"I thought you'd never ask. Roberto and Maria went to Bloomington and are staying out for dinner, so I happen to be free. I just finished baking pies, and—" A loud knock on the front door interrupted me. "Hang on, somebody's here. I should be able to get rid of them. The restaurant sign is turned to CLOSED, and the B&B sign has FULL hanging below it." I spoke as I walked toward the door. "Oh, nuts," I muttered.

"What is it?" Abe asked.

"It's somebody in a brown and tan uniform, that's what."

"The county sheriff's department uniform."

"Then she's either the detective conducting the investigation into Pia's murder or one of her helpers. I'd better talk to her. What time are you picking me up?"

"Six-thirty give you enough time?"

"Sure, thanks." I lowered my own voice. "But I'll tell her five-thirty." I disconnected to the sound of Abe's laugh and unlocked the double bolts.

Chapter Twelve

The officer, a slender woman with a long black braid hanging down her back, had introduced herself as Detective Sergeant Anne Henderson, the lead detective in the sheriff's department. Her flat-brimmed hat looked like the ones the National Park Service rangers wore, and the tan necktie and epaulets contrasting with her dark brown shirt matched her tan pants. All of which looked crisp and freshly pressed, despite it being near the end of what had to have been a long day for her.

I'd put on a fresh pot of coffee, and we'd already been through two rounds of the same questions while I did prep for tomorrow morning. I'd told her what time Roberto and Maria and I had come home yesterday and what time they'd left. Same for Chase, at least as far as I knew. I'd said—at least twice—I'd only seen Abe onstage yesterday, and no, I didn't think his minor quarrel with Pia, amplified though it was, was anything he'd commit murder over. I repeated—again, twice—what I'd told Buck of Sue and the money she'd said Pia owed her.

"Lieutenant Bird said you aren't aware of your guests' comings and goings," Detective Henderson said. Her deep brown eyes were almond shaped and her high cheekbones made me think she was part Shawnee or descended from the Miami tribe farther to the north in Indiana, despite the very British-sounding surname of Henderson. "It doesn't seem like a particularly secure situation. Are you sure that's a good idea?"

Ack. I cocked my head. "I hadn't thought about it. This is the first week the bed-and-breakfast rooms have been occupied, actually. I don't know what else I could do other than hire someone to be awake all night, or sleep upstairs myself."

"I might recommend you install a camera on the outside egress. That way you can at least monitor your guests' movements."

A camera. Why hadn't I considered a camera? Installing one might not be a bad idea, and they probably sold ones you could access through an app. "Good idea. I hadn't thought of a camera. Thanks."

She bobbed her head in acknowledgment. "But since you don't have one, we're going to need to interview all your guests regarding what they heard in the night. Lieutenant Bird neglected to ask all the questions I would have liked him to. Let's see." She checked her tablet. "I have the Italians' names and Mr. Fracasso's number, and Mr. Broward's contact information. Who else is staying in your rooms?"

I told her Beth's and Ed's names, and extracted their cell phone numbers from my own phone.

"Thank you. Lieutenant Bird mentioned that you overheard Ms. Ferguson expressing dislike of the victim."

"I did. But just briefly. Detective, how was Pia killed? I know Isaac found her body, but was she shot? Poisoned? Stabbed?" I paused in my assembly of the dry ingredients for pancake batter.

She tapped her hand on the end of the counter where she'd laid her tablet. "I hear you've acted as an amateur detective previously."

"Not exactly. I simply kept getting drawn into murder cases." I shrugged.

"I'll tell you the method, but first I'd like your word that this time you won't get 'drawn into' my investigation." She surrounded the words in finger quotes.

"Fine with me," I answered. But was it?

"Ms. Bianchi was choked. Garroted, actually."

Garroted? "You mean with a rope or something?" A shudder rippled through me at the thought.

"It was actually a metal wire. We're looking into whether it was an instrument string, and if so, designed for which instrument."

"Wow. With thousands of musicians in the county this week."

"Exactly." She nodded slowly, frowning. "It won't be an easy case, but most homicides aren't. I will ask that you keep this information to yourself. We're trying to keep it from disseminating to the public."

"Not a problem." I worked for a minute, measuring baking powder for pancakes and adding it to the flour already in the bowl. "Here's something you haven't asked me. It happened after Buck left here this morning."

"Yes?"

I added the salt to the flour. "When you called Sue Berry into the station, she phoned asking me to contact Glen, her husband. I got through to him eventually, and he didn't seem to like Pia at all."

"Oh?" The detective's long, smooth-skinned fingers paused above the keyboard on her tablet.

"Yes. Glen even called her a slut."

The detective's eyebrows went way up.

I set the pancake mix aside and measured out flour for biscuits. "He said Pia and Sue sang in choir together. Or no, maybe they went to the same church? Anyway, he thought Pia should sing in the choir with Sue instead of spending a lot of money on the IU music department. Something like that. Whatever, it's more information for you. I know by now every little fact can help, even if people don't think it's important."

She nodded. "You got that right. Now, to confirm. You have no knowledge of Abraham O'Neill's whereabouts late last night or before dawn this morning?"

Gah. "No, I'm afraid not. He went to his house last night and I slept here."

"He said as much. Pity no one can vouch for him. Considering his public altercation with the victim."

I set floury fists on my waist. "I was in the audience, Detective. It was hardly an altercation. More like a disagreement over a playlist. You don't murder people over something like a song."

"You and I don't. Some might." Her expression was calm. This woman was indeed all business.

"Not Abe O'Neill. Never." I headed toward the walk-in. "Hang on a sec, I have to get a few things." I returned, arms full holding a pound of butter, a dozen eggs, and a gallon of milk.

"Now tell me more about your guest Chase Broward. Your"—she checked her notes—"friend Philostrate MacDonald is a classmate of the victim, and he said Mr. Broward had a romantic relationship with the deceased, his marriage notwithstanding. Is this correct?"

I nodded as I cut butter into the biscuit flour. The detective had pronounced Phil's name the same way Phil and his grandfather Samuel did. They both said it in four syllables, with *stra* being the next to last followed by *tay*. In my mind, I did, too, although of course I just called him Phil.

Detective Henderson cocked her head and scrunched up her nose. "Off the record, what in the world kind of name is Philostrate? Sounds like Greek pastry or something."

I laughed and started to crack eggs into a well in the biscuit mix. "It's a Greek name. Shakespeare used it, and I think other writers did, too. But we call him Phil. Have you talked to him yet?"

"Still trying to reach him. Speaking of that, I'd better get on the road." She stood. "I have an appointment in Bloomington in an hour, and I'm sure you have things to do, too."

"As a matter of fact, I do." Even though, thanks to her not minding that I worked while we talked, much of my prep was done.

"Please don't hesitate to contact me with any new information. Ms. Jordan, Lieutenant Bird as well as

Oscar Thompson have informed me of your role in several homicides over the last year. I trust by now you know to leave the detection to the professionals, correct?"

I felt like using Danna and Turner's favorite affectionate phrase, "You're the boss, boss," but I restrained myself. "Absolutely. And Detective?"

"Yes?"

"Good luck."

She nodded her head an inch in acknowledgment. "I appreciate that. Thanks for the coffee."

Chapter Thirteen

I held the door until she left, then double locked it again. I couldn't be too careful with a murderer at large. I unlocked and opened the door to my apartment so Birdy could keep me company as I worked and thought. He streaked into the restaurant, then began a serious cleaning atop a butter churn in the vintage cookware area. I quick-kneaded the biscuit dough and stored it, tightly wrapped, in the walk-in.

After I cleaned up, I pondered what to do next. I could go into my own private space, put my feet up, enjoy a glass of an adult beverage, and play with my kitty. Definitely a good plan for the next fifty minutes until Abe picked me up.

But for the first time since I'd opened my B&B four days ago, none of my guests were in their rooms and none were expected back for hours. I had the master key, of course, even though they each held individual room keys. And what if Chase Broward had killed his erstwhile lover? Shouldn't I look for clues and let the police know? My inner nag scolded me that I could have invited the detective to check the room ten minutes ago when she was right here in my store. But surely she'd need a search warrant or something to make it legal. Whereas little old inn-keeper me? I had the key and I owned the building.

I retrieved the master key from the back of my desk drawer where it lived in an envelope cleverly la-beled Key to Shed—even though I didn't actually have a shed—and off I trotted. Upstairs I first peeked into the Rose room, where I'd put my father and his wife. I didn't know if this was Roberto or Maria's doing—maybe both—but the bed was neatly made and the room was almost tidier than before they'd arrived. One closed suitcase rested on the vintage luggage rack I'd rescued and refurbished, and only a tidy stack of tourism folders and maps sat on the edge of the desk. Their house in Italy had always been neat, too, when I'd gone to visit in late December.

The Rose room was a lovely one, if I did say so myself. I'd decided it was easiest to name each room after its color scheme. Rose print wallpaper, an an-tique four-poster bed, and simple muslin curtains with rose-colored tiebacks were the main decora-tions. I'd found and had sent to be cleaned a muted purple and blue braided rug to sit atop the finished wide-pine floors, original to the building. A wooden rocker in the corner featured a cushion covered in the same fabric as the quilted coverlet.

But I wasn't here to admire my interior-decorating prowess. I backed out, locked the door, and glanced into Ed and Beth's room. The Sapphire room I'd done in a blue theme, but you could hardly tell. Clothes, books, and shoes were scattered everywhere. The bedcover hung half on the floor. The blinds were down and I could tell the windows were closed by the musky scent within. Yeah, I knew what they'd been doing all morning. Once again I backed out and locked the door, feeling for underpaid hotel maids everywhere who had to tidy up such messes as part of their daily work.

Only the Emerald room to go. As I eased open Chase's door, a business card fell to the floor. He must have wedged it in the gap between the door and the jamb so he could tell if anyone intruded. I shivered. If that didn't seem like the mark of a guilty person, I don't know what did. I examined the card. Maybe one of the other musicians had left it for him. But no, it was one of his own.

I took one step into the Emerald room and heard a creak behind me. I froze. Had someone broken into the store? Maybe I hadn't locked the service door. Had Chase come home early with the aim of catching me going through his things? I whirled, heart thudding against my ribs.

And laughed out loud. Birdy, sitting on a rather frail hall table, was furiously bathing, one hind leg up next to his head. The table creaked with every movement. I scooped up my cat and deposited him onto the stairs, stepping back up and closing the door to the upstairs so he couldn't sneak up here again. I firmly admonished my heart to calm down before resuming my quest.

Chase's green-decorated room was a middle ground between the other two. His bed was unmade but nothing littered the floor. I spied a couple bumper of stickers on the desk. One blared DON'T BE A COWARD, VOTE FOR BROWARD with *US Senate* below in smaller

letters. The other read CUT TO THE CHASE WITH
BROWARD FOR SENATE. He must be trying out slogans
for the Senate run. I pulled open the closet door and
found no surprises there. A western-style shirt with
musical clefs and guitars in the print. A pair of tennis
shoes. Creased jeans on a hanger. *Huh?* Who ironed
their jeans? I shut the door.

I wasn't sure what I was expecting to find in
here. A little stylized hand pointing to a certain
spot, lettered with *Evidence Here*? I turned to leave. I
didn't want to waste any more of my precious relax-
ation time. Still—why had he wedged his card in the
door if he wasn't expecting an intruder? And if he
was, why? I stood in the middle of the room and closed
my eyes, letting the feeling of the room wash over
me. I was normally a logic-driven kind of girl, but I'd
discovered over the last couple months that a moment
of mindfulness could do wonders for quieting the busy
brain and letting solutions find their way in.

When I opened my eyes, my gaze landed on the
schoolroom desk I'd refurbished. And the white
wicker wastebasket on the floor next to it. I glimpsed
the word *Gibson* sticking out and I stepped over to see
what it was. *Gibson Signature Series* headed a square
piece of paper the size of a piece of toast. I stared at
a picture of Earl Scruggs playing a banjo, and at the
words *Banjo Strings*. Except Chase played the guitar,
not the banjo.

Chapter Fourteen

I sat holding Abe's hand facing the music park's main stage a couple hours later. We perched in his matching folding camp chairs, the arms of which included drink holders. His held a big cup of hard cider, mine a cold Pilsner. At least you could buy alcohol at the park; in fact it featured an entire beer pavilion. We'd demolished the picnic supper he'd brought. You couldn't go wrong with cold chicken drumsticks and skewers of cherry tomatoes, small mozzarella balls, and pitted kalamata olives, plus a sliced sourdough baguette. All finger food, all delicious. And I hadn't had to prepare any of it, or clean up, for that matter. He'd promised dessert once we'd digested our dinner. By dessert I couldn't tell if he meant a stop at the ice cream stand or a roll in the hay—or both.

The group onstage, a rollicking jug band, had finished. Everywhere around us I could still hear music. A jug band off to the left, the thrum of dueling banjos behind us, a lilting fiddle tune to our right. Live music was definitely not confined to the

stage. A cool breeze gave a welcome respite from the
day's warm air, and wafted the scent of some sweet
blooming flower past us.

"Who's up next?" I asked.

He pulled out a program. "Looks like they're called
Corrine Pie and Spice." He extended the program for
me to see.

My eyes widened. *Could it be?* "Don't tell me Danna's
mom has a bluegrass band. The mayor of South Lick
also plays music?"

A little smile played with his mouth but he kept it
under control. "Guess you'll have to wait and see."

I batted his arm with the program and settled in
to let the flow of the crowd and the music from the
sidelines wash over me, grateful for no more de-
mands on my time than just being. New musicians
filed onto the stage and started tuning up.

I pictured the banjo string package in Chase's
wastebasket. "Hey, Abe?"

"Hey, Robbie."

"What's the difference between guitar strings and
banjo strings?"

"That's a topic of much debate in these circles.
Some say music wire is music wire and that they're
interchangeable. Both instruments can use either
plain steel wire or wrapped-wire strings, and some
use a mix of both."

"But don't they have different, um, tunings or
something?"

Abe laughed at me and I elbowed him.

"I don't know anything about music," I protested.

"I realize that, sweetheart. I'm just ribbing you.
To answer your question, the strings are always

packaged separately and some say that's for a reason. But if I happened to wreck all my banjo strings and the only replacements were for guitar, I'd use the guitar strings."

Huh. So that wrapper in Chase's room could be perfectly innocent. Maybe he had run out of guitar strings and the only ones available were for the banjo. Then I pictured the business card he had wedged in his door and I sucked air in through a grimace. I never put it back. *Gah.* He could be a hundred percent crime-free and still not want anyone in his room. What if he noticed the card was gone? Except by invitation, nobody could have gone in his room except him and me unless he'd left his door unlocked. If he asked, I'd bluff through it, saying I was emptying wastebaskets. Except that I hadn't emptied his. I'd just have to hope he was the non-observant type.

At the strum of a guitar and a banjo arpeggio, Corrine Beedle, the mayor of South Lick, strode onto the stage, guitar slung across her red satin shirt tucked into black leather pants. Her red high-heeled cowboy boots boosted her height to at least six foot two. Corrine never did anything halfway.

She adjusted the standing mike up to her level. "Howdy, everybody! How y'all doing?"

A few shouts of "Awesome" and "Howdy" floated up.

"I can't hear you." Corrine broadcast her wide toothy smile as she drew out the *hear.* "I said, how y'all doing?"

This time nearly everybody shouted, "Great!"

"Now that's more like it. I'm Corrine Pie, and this here's my all-girl band, Spice. Let's give the girls a big ol' welcome." She started the applause as three female musicians holding instruments—a fiddle, a mandolin, and a banjo—trooped onstage. Sue Berry followed them, bringing up the rear.

"Before we get some tunes rolling for y'all, our fabulous organizer, Ms. Sue Berry, has something sad to share."

The crowd quieted while Corrine slid the mike down a foot for Sue, who was even shorter than me.

"You may have heard," Sue began with a quaver in her voice, "we lost one of our fine local musicians and friends last night. Let's all hold a moment of silence for Pia Bianchi, may she rest in peace in God's arms." Sue pressed her lips together as she bowed her head.

Judging from what Glen had told me, Pia and Sue had been friends before the loan came between them. Despite her anger at Pia last night, Sue seemed to be suffering the loss. It couldn't have helped to be hauled into the police station in the middle of it, but at least they'd let her go. I hoped I'd have a minute to talk with her tonight.

Abe squeezed my hand and closed his eyes. I kept the silence, but gazed around the crowd. Most in the audience had bowed their heads, too. A woman near me moved her lips in silent prayer. A man crossed himself. Off to my right, leaning against a tall fir tree, stood Chase Broward, eyes also open. He spotted me looking at him and raised his chin in acknowledgment. No silent prayer for Pia from him. I had snapped a couple of cell phone pictures of the banjo string wrapper in his wastebasket without touching it and texted them to Detective Henderson. It could be something perfectly innocent. For all I knew he also played banjo and had left it in his car.

Sue murmured, "Thank you, and God bless," before walking with shoulders bowed into the wings.

"All righty," Corrine leaned down to say, bringing the microphone back up to her level. "I want to ask one of our good friends to come up onstage to help us ladies get this set underway. Mister Chase Broward, you out there?" She shielded her eyes from the lights and perused the crowd. A minute later, my guest bounded up the steps holding his guitar, waved to the audience, and gave Corrine a big hug.

"This gentleman's gonna be our next United States Senator, y'all. Let's give him a big ol' hand!"

The audience roared their approval, and the applause only died down when the strumming started up.

I stretched my legs out. "That was interesting."

"Which part?" Abe asked.

"All of it. Corrine having an all-female band. You knew, didn't you?"

He smiled, nodding. "You know, Brown County is a village. All the musicians know each other."

"I'm also a bit surprised Sue was looking torn up over Pia's death. She was pretty angry at Pia yesterday."

"Doesn't mean she isn't grieving the loss of a friend."

"I guess. And then Corrine introducing Chase as the next senator. I didn't think he had started his campaign yet, but apparently he has."

"Politicians." Abe gave a little eye roll, but his foot was tapping to the music.

"You should be up there playing." I nudged his elbow. "You're better than Senator Broward." Chase was playing well, but from what I could hear, it was a pretty simple tune.

"Nah. I'm taking the night off to be with my best girl." He leaned over and planted a lazy kiss on my cheek.

"Without Pia," I said softly.

"May she rest in peace in God's arms, as Sue said."

I squeezed his hand. He wasn't any more attached to an organized religion than I was, but I knew he harbored a strong faith in kindness and generosity of spirit. It showed in everything he did.

Chapter Fifteen

Onstage the music flowed into a slower number. Chase gave a salute to Corrine and slipped into the wings. Off to the left of the seating area I spied Sue standing with Danna and somebody else in the long shadows of the end of the day.

"I'm going to run say hi to Sue," I said to Abe. "I want to see how she's doing. Okay?"

"Of course." Abe lifted his cider cup. "A refill on your way back?"

"You bet." I wove through the sea of chairs and legs until I reached a roped-off passageway, then made my way toward Sue and Danna. Clipboard in hand again, Sue looked somber but her eyes weren't red or puffy. Maybe I'd been mistaken about the depth of her grief. Or maybe she'd swallowed it down because running the show had a more urgent priority.

"Hey, Robbie," Danna said when I walked up. "I want you to meet someone."

The small group included a big man with a full beard, shaved head, and a gentle expression. His arm lay across Danna's back, a tattoo of an anvil decorating his forearm.

"Robbie, this is Isaac Rowling," Danna said. "Isaac, meet my boss, Robbie Jordan."

I shook his hand, but mine felt lost in his bear paw. "So pleased to meet you, Isaac. I've heard a lot about you."

"I'm in trouble now," he said with a smile.

I stared at his eyes, one brown and one green. His lashes were longer, fuller, and curlier than even Corrine's in full makeup. I tore my gaze away to greet Sue.

"How are you holding up?" I asked.

She lifted her chin a little. "I'm all right. Our lawyer was able to extricate me from the detective's clutches today. She couldn't hold me. She doesn't have any evidence, because I didn't kill Pia over no stupid loan." She blew out a frustrated breath. "She sure as heck ruined my day, though."

"Tell me about it," Isaac said. "Down at the station they seemed to think because my dog and me found that lady's body, I had something to do with her death. The poor thing."

"I'm sorry you had to go through that," I said. "Finding the body, I mean."

"Yeah. Robbie knows. She found a dead body right in our store after Thanksgiving last year," Danna added. She glanced at Sue with a quick intake of breath and brought her hand to her mouth. "Oh, I'm so sorry, Ms. Berry. I wasn't thinking."

The body I'd found had been Sue's daughter. Another reason why Sue never would have murdered someone else. She knew what anguish the loved ones went through afterward.

Sue pressed her eyes closed for a moment, then opened them, swiping away a tear. "It's okay. I have lots of good memories of her. I know it was rough on you, Robbie."

"It was. It's shocking and scary and really hard." I pictured finding Erica next to my pickle barrel and shuddered. "How are you doing after discovering Pia in the bridge?" I asked Isaac.

"It was kinda of tough. I mean, I grew up hunting, so it's not like I've never seen a dead body. But a person? That's different. Reminded me of being deployed."

"Did you recognize her? Did you know who she was?" I asked.

Isaac looked out over my head for a second or two.

"You met her at a contra dance, right, Ize?" Danna prodded.

"Right. Then she bought one of my metal sculptures and wanted to pay in installments. Except she stopped paying."

"Really?" Sue's eyebrows went up. "She did the same thing to me. Not for a sculpture, of course, but on a loan I gave her."

"She must really have been hard up for cash," Danna said, stroking Isaac's arm. "Did you try to make her give you what she owed you?"

In front of my eyes Isaac withdrew into himself. It was hardly anything physical. It was more that the expression on his face went flat.

"Are you saying I hurt her?" he asked, his voice also devoid of feeling.

"Of course not. Don't be silly," Danna scoffed. "I mean, did you, like, call her, or write her an e-mail saying she still owed you? That's all I meant."

If I hadn't been watching Isaac closely, I would have missed his face returning to normal.

"Of course. I sent her a second bill, and a third. But it wasn't a huge amount of money." He made a small waving gesture with his big hand as if the debt was so inconsequential it could be brushed away like a cobweb.

I hesitated with my next question, but my urge to know won over. "Don't answer this if you don't want to, Isaac, but I'm curious. Do you have any idea if Pia had recently died, or if she'd been there a long time?"

"The detective asked me the same question. I don't know the answer. I thought I should see if she had a pulse, even though I couldn't believe she could with the, um, wire around her neck." He shivered, which for an instant made him seem much smaller and younger than he was. "Her skin was cold. That's all I know."

"A wire?" I asked.

"Yeah, almost like a guitar or banjo string."

Garroted. Exactly what Henderson had told me. If Pia's skin was cold, she could have been killed the night before or an hour before. Henderson and her team would have analyzed how stiff the body was and where. I thought they usually could tell within a two- or three-hour window of time.

Isaac went on. "And then, the police acted like they were suspecting me—me!—after I thought I had done

the right thing by borrowing the minister's phone."
He gave a quick shake of his head.

"I heard about that," I said. "You didn't have your
cell on you?"

"I did, but I forgot to charge it last night. I've
walked by the sign that's posted down there lots of
times. I didn't want to leave the lady lying there
alone, but I didn't have a choice."

"There's no traffic on the bridge road early in the
morning, anyway," Danna added.

The bridge road hardly had any traffic at any
time of day. Poor Pia. Dying at the hands of someone she probably knew, but otherwise alone. At
night. On a lonely road.

The music changed again to an energetic fast-
paced tune, and I shook off the image, focusing
instead on the performers onstage. "Since when
does your mom have a bluegrass group?" I asked
Danna.

Danna tossed her head. "She's completely nuts. As
if being mayor doesn't keep her busy. Anyway, she's
always played the guitar, but only at home. Then she
met the mandolin player last year, the one up onstage?" She pointed. "It was during a jam session at
last year's festival and they got to talking. Next thing
I knew Mom's hosting rehearsals in our living room.
It's okay. Keeps her out of trouble."

"Glen plays guitar, too," Sue said with a fond look
on her face. "But classical guitar, and sometimes jazz.
He likes to go out in the woods early in the morning
to practice. He has this bench in a clearing behind
our house where he sets, or he'll drive somewhere
else to practice. Says he likes to play the sun up."

"He told me he can't stand bluegrass," I said.

"Funny, isn't it?" Sue said. "I love it, and then I get this job. Well, God made the world a big place for a reason, right?"

Isaac lightly tugged Danna's elbow.

"I'm coming, I'm coming." She smiled at Sue and me. "The man loves to dance. So do I. See you in the morning, Robbie."

"Danna, by the way, I got all the pies made, and managed to do the breakfast prep, too," I said.

"Sweet."

"Have fun, kids," I said, then wondered why I'd said *kids*. I was less than ten years older than Danna. Owning my own business, being responsible for everything, made me feel older. "I'm headed to the beer pavilion," I said to Sue as the couple walked away.

"And I have to run over and check the Hippy Hill stage, make sure everything's running smooth. You take care, now." She bustled away, too.

But when I came back, cider and beer in hand, Sue was nowhere near the Hippy Hill stage. Instead, she stood huddled with Chase at the back of the audience watching the main stage. I couldn't see hers or Chase's face, but body language said he was trying to convince her of something, and she wasn't having any part of it.

Chapter Sixteen

"You two rocking the concert?" Phil asked half an hour later, sinking gracefully down to sit cross-legged in front of Abe and me, beer in hand.

"Great tunes," Abe said. "How's it going, man?"

The musicians on the stage now, two men and two women, all siblings, were singing some amazing harmonies, even as they also played a fiddle, a guitar, a bass, and a banjo. I figured there had to be something about familial voices that made their music so much more compelling.

"Just fine," Phil replied. He tapped his hand against his knee in time with the music.

"You seem to like all kinds of music, Phil, not only opera," I said.

"Of course! Music is the food of the soul. There's no bad style, no genre I don't like."

I scrunched my nose. "I don't like jazz much, at least some of it. It can sound, I don't know, discordant? It jars me."

Phil nodded. "I know what you mean. But that's the really creative stuff, riffing, improvising."

I cocked my head. "Do you know Glen Berry? He said he loves jazz."

"The liquor store guy?" Phil frowned a little. "Sure, I know him. Kind of an odd bird, don't you think?"

"How so?" Abe asked.

"I don't know," Phil went on. "All smiles, all the time. But maybe not real smiles? You know the type?"

I nodded. "I hadn't really gotten that impression from him. I don't suppose either of you ever saw him and Pia together, did you?"

"Now that you mention it," Abe began, "I saw them in a car last week. I was out in Gnaw Bone fixing a line, and they were sitting parked to the side of the little food place."

I gazed at him. "Interesting." I filed it away in a list of pieces to this puzzle. "Just sitting there, not, like, making out or anything?"

Abe laughed. "Why would you think that?"

"I'm curious, too," Phil added.

"It was something Glen told me. He said Pia was a slut."

"Interesting," Abe said.

"I know," I said. "Sue had befriended Pia and asked her over to dinner one night. Glen had to drive her home. Maybe she came on to him."

"When I saw them it looked like they were arguing," Abe offered.

"I saw Pia more than once with the Broward dude," Phil said. "And they definitely weren't arguing. The car windows were literally steaming up."

"Where did you see them?" I asked.

"Here and there. In a campus parking lot near the IU music department. In the Bloomingfoods parking lot. Over in South Lick by the gazebo."

I frowned. "Those last two are really public places, right out in the open."

"Yeah. I don't think she cared if they were seen, but I was surprised he didn't. Public office holder and married, too." He smiled with a sad expression. "Pia, she was so full of life. I really liked her, despite her hanging with a married man. She was the definition of exuberant. It came across in her singing, too."

"The flip side of exuberance, at least in Pia, was her temper." Abe shook his head. "That woman was a volcano ready to erupt."

I shivered. The night air was cooling, and I pulled my denim jacket closer around me. But I shivered partly at the thought of Pia's tempestuous life ending so abruptly, so violently. And partly at the idea that whoever murdered her was still wandering among us.

The music changed to a waltz. Abe jumped up and offered me his hand. "May I have this dance, miss?"

I smiled. Exactly the antidote I needed. I let myself be hoisted out of my chair. "See you, Phil."

He smiled back and also pushed up to standing. "I'd better go find me a lady to waltz with."

But as Abe steered me expertly through steps, the lilting tune only accentuated the confusing pieces forming the Pia puzzle, as I'd started thinking of it. The list of clues was getting longer, but I wasn't filling in the acrosses and downs of the crossword very fast. Not at all, actually.

I shook my head and came back to the present. I didn't need to solve the puzzle. That was the detective's profession, her main job. All I had to do was text her what I'd seen and learned tonight. I succeeded in losing myself to Abe, to the music, to the dance. At least for right now.

Chapter Seventeen

Six-thirty today felt earlier this morning than some days, since Abe and I hadn't gotten home until ten, and we'd had the delectable dessert of each other to enjoy. He'd been up and off to his job by five-thirty as he always was when he stayed over on a week-night.

I was showered, dressed, and in the store, turning sausages as the coffee brewed when Danna waltzed in. Literally. She was humming "Brand New Tennessee Waltz," the same song Abe and I had danced to last night.

"Don't mind me." She grinned, twirling as she approached the kitchen. "I think I found my new favorite dance." Her vintage dress, a rayon with sprays of blue and green flowers, twirled with her.

"Abe and I danced to that, too." I poured coffee into a mug and handed it to her, then poured for myself. "It's lovely, isn't it?"

"You bet. Thanks for the brew." She sipped it and then set it down. Still humming, she tied on a store apron and set to work setting the tables.

"You two had fun last night, then." In California, I didn't know any high school and college students who enjoyed bluegrass, but Danna seemed to love it. Maybe it was the effect of growing up with the music all around her, which I hadn't.

"We did. For such a big guy, Isaac's a light-footed dancer."

I began cracking eggs into a mixing bowl, prepping for omelets and scrambled eggs, but thinking of Isaac. "Remind me how long you've known him."

"I met him this winter, but we were only a bunch of friends doing fun stuff. He and I started hanging out in March."

"Do you feel like you know him pretty well?"

She filled a tray with the caddies of condiments we put on each table. "What do you mean?" she asked without looking at me.

My radar sent up an alarm. "Do you trust him?"

"Robbie!" Danna whirled and strode toward me. "Do you mean do I think he killed Pia? Of course not. Of course I trust him. He's a good man. He's sweet to me. What's not to trust?"

"Whoa, hang on there. I was simply asking." I held up both hands palms out.

"But why?" She folded her arms and stared down at me. Corrine's daughter all the way, right down to the tall gene.

"Last night there was a minute when his face got weird," I said. "Funny, like blank. And it was when you asked him if he'd tried to get his money out of Pia. You didn't see it?"

The ire went out of Danna's face, replaced by a furrowed brow and pursed lips. She took a deep breath and let it out. "Of course I did. He's done it before. Robbie, he has some kind of secret, some dark thing in his past. I've asked him what's going on inside when it happens but he won't tell me. He's a veteran, so maybe it has to do with his experiences when he was deployed."

PTSD? I only nodded.

"It never lasts very long, though. And I do trust him. You should, too."

Her intuitions had always been spot on about people. Still, I thought it bore digging a little deeper into Isaac's past. What if his dark secret was pathological? Bursts of violence? Homicidal tendencies? I hoped the sheriff would look into Isaac's past. A sausage spit a drop of hot grease, but I raised my hand fast enough to avoid it. I turned each over, and the smell of browned meat proved irresistible, so I forked up one and waved it to cool in the air.

"I trust you, and that counts for a lot." I glanced down, spotting a tattooed anklet on her right lower leg. "Since when do you have a tat?" I bit off the end of the sausage, savoring the smoky maple flavor.

She blushed. "I went with Ize last week. I've always wanted one. Do you like it?" She lifted her foot and rotated her ankle, showing off the strands of the interwoven inked-in chain.

"It's lovely." Not for me, but it looked nice on her. "Now, any ideas for a breakfast special?"

Her expression lightened. "I was considering specials on the way over. We should make something from Kentucky. Bluegrass, right?"

"I've heard of the Hot Brown sandwich, but we'd

need to order in turkey breast and then make the Mornay sauce ahead of time."

"Yeah," Danna said. "Let's do the sandwiches for a lunch special tomorrow."

"How about fried apples for today? I know we have a bunch of Granny Smiths in the cooler."

"Ooh, apples fried in butter? Great idea." She hurried over to the Specials board and wrote Hot Butter-Fried Apples. "I think we have a container of boiled potatoes in the walk-in, too. What if I also list Bluegrass Omelet, and say it's with country ham and potatoes?"

"Go for it."

We worked in silence for a few minutes, my mind roving over last evening. "Danna, how does your mom know Chase Broward? You know, the guy staying upstairs."

Danna wrinkled her nose as she thought. "I think she said she met him at a city government meeting. Because she's the mayor and he's a city councillor in Bloomington."

"She acted last night like she supports his run for Senate."

"Who knows? Maybe that was only for show."

By the time we opened at seven, the apples were sizzling, I had the potatoes all diced and ready to go, and was cubing thick slices of ham. After the bell on the door jangled, Wanda Bird walked in. I did a double take. Buck's cousin was uniformed, all right, but her uniform was brown over tan, exactly like the sheriff's detective yesterday, not the dark blue of the South Lick Police she'd worn the last time I talked with her back in the winter.

"Howdy Robbie, Danna," she said.

"Hey, Wanda. Hungry?" I called. "Sit anywhere."

She approached us and stood feet apart, hand on the gun in a holster attached to her three-inch-wide duty belt. Her robust female figure strained the sheriff's uniform as much as it had that of the local department. She'd slicked her strawberry blond hair back into a bun as severely as it always was. A shiny badge decorated the short-sleeved shirt above a name tag reading DETECTIVE W. BIRD, which was pinned above the pocket on the left breast, literally in her case. A blue and gold star-shaped cloth patch had been sewn onto the left pocket, which read SHERIFF DEPT, BROWN COUNTY, IND.

"Since when are you with the county sheriff's department?" I asked. "Last I knew you were working for Buck right here in South Lick."

"Well, opportunity called and I answered. Turns out the sheriff's department had an opening for a deputy detective, and I went for it. More possibility for advancement. And after helping Buck out a few times on those cases you were involved in, I realized I liked investigative work. Plus, it's kind of nice working for a lady for a change."

I tilted my head. Her local accent had all but disappeared. On purpose, or had she been putting it on before?

"Anyway, I would like to eat," she said. "But we have a couple few more questions for you, Robbie. The boss asked me to come on out and set with you a piece."

Or maybe her accent wasn't gone, after all. I'd never heard *couple few* used anywhere but in southern Indiana. Same with *might could* and *should oughta,* along with *set with you a piece.*

Wanda went on. "Hoped the place would be nice and quiet like it is. Can you spare a minute?"

Not really. But I didn't voice the thought. I finished laying bacon on the griddle and caught Danna's gaze. "I'll only be a minute."

Danna nodded and took over at the stove.

I beckoned to Wanda and headed toward my desk area in the corner. "What's up?"

"Anne, that is, Detective Henderson said you texted her last night you learned something. I'm here to find out what it was."

"I wanted to tell her a couple things I found out last night. I was over in Beanblossom listening to music." I half perched on my desk. "Sit down if you want."

"It's okay." She brushed away my offer. "I was at the music park, too. Heared some pretty great pickin' and a couple talented fiddlers. Didn't see y'all."

"I'm not surprised. You know how many people were there. Anyway, you know Phil MacDonald, right?"

"Of course."

"And I'm sure you must know he and Pia were both students in the IU music department. He still is, of course." At Wanda's nod I went on. "He told me he saw Pia and Chase Broward together a few times. Getting, well, extra-friendly in a car. I'm sure he'll be happy to tell you where and when."

Her pale, almost unnoticeable blond eyebrows went up nearly to her hairline. "I'll contact him about what he saw. For now, give me the bullet points. So to speak." She pulled a small notebook and pen out of a pocket on her belt.

I let her know the three places Phil had mentioned seeing the couple. "I told Detective Henderson yesterday what Glen Berry said about Pia. Well, it turns out Abe spied them in a car together in Gnaw Bone. And they weren't being all lovey-dovey like her and Chase. On the contrary, Abe thought they were arguing."

"Duly noted." She scribbled. "Anything else?"

I checked that Danna was occupied at the griddle and turned my back on her, lowering my voice. "Has the investigation already looked into Isaac Rowling's past?"

Wanda narrowed her eyes. "Somebody's on that. Not sure what he dug up."

"Danna said he has a dark side. Last night he said Pia had bought a metal sculpture from him but hadn't given him the full amount she owed for it. When Danna asked if he'd tried to make Pia pay, his face went strange, expressionless. I don't know if it means anything, but it's a point of information."

"Thanks. We have noted he's a veteran. The smallest little thing can trigger PTSD, you know. Anything else?"

"Not at the moment. No, wait. Sue Berry and Chase Broward seemed to be arguing about something last night. I didn't hear the words. It was just their body language from a distance." I felt like there was something else I was missing, but I couldn't place what. Was that all I'd learned? No. I could tell her what I'd seen in the Emerald room, even though I'd already sent the pictures to Henderson. I didn't know how closely they communicated or if the detective had even seen my text. She hadn't acknowledged it. "I have one more thing."

Wanda's stomach complained audibly of hunger. "Hope it's quick. I'm so hungry I'm fartin' cobwebs."

I snorted. Wanda was plenty of things, but dainty wasn't among them. "I was freshening the rooms yesterday after Detective Henderson left." I mentally crossed my fingers at the lie. "In Chase Broward's room I saw a banjo string wrapper. And he plays the guitar. I don't know if it's important or not, but it could be. I took some pictures and texted them to the detective."

"Got it. Why would he go and have a thing like that?"

"Abe told me you can use banjo strings on the guitar, but most musicians would only do that as a last resort."

"I hear ya." She jotted something down, then stashed her pen and notebook. "Now for some grub. I'll take both of them there specials and a plate of biscuits and gravy with a side of bacon, if you don't mind."

"Why would I mind?" Her appetite was almost as legendary as Buck's, but the cousins were like Jack Sprat and his wife, not that skinny Buck avoided fat—on the contrary. It just never turned to fat on his body, unlike what happened to the rest of the known universe, including Wanda and me.

Wanda laughed. "Gotta keep up my girlish figure, you know." She patted her hefty hips with a grin.

She was a woman happy with her self-image, despite not being anywhere near the body America's advertising giants would have us all believe was ideal. Mine wasn't either, with my curvy hips, although on top I wasn't particularly busty, unlike Wanda. I was content with my shape, too.

Chapter Eighteen

Roberto and Maria came downstairs while Wanda was eagerly attacking her triple breakfast. A few more customers had dropped in, but we were still pretty quiet. I greeted my father and his wife with kisses on both cheeks.

"How was Bloomington, *Babbo*? Did you visit all your old haunts?" I asked, smiling.

"We did. I showed Maria everything, *è giusto, cara*?"

Maria agreed in Italian, but she shot me a quick eye roll. I was getting to really like this woman.

"We eat at Nick's," she said.

"You ate at Nick's English Hut?" A hangout favored by students, professors, and townies alike and only a block from the main entrance into campus, it offered great beer, above-average pub fare, and a true Bloomington ambiance.

Roberto beamed. "But of course. The town, she has changed much, no?"

"It must have, in twenty-seven years." It had to have changed considerably. After his quarry accident, Roberto's last days in the state had been spent in University Hospital, unfortunately. I hoped he hadn't included the big health-care facility on his tour. "Sit down and let me bring you breakfast. We can go over today's plans while it's quiet. Remember, I'm taking you out to Hoosier Hollow for dinner. It's right here in South Lick, and we can even walk there. My friend Christina is the head chef." Every dish at the upscale restaurant was delicious and prepared with caring expertise.

"Abe comes too?" Maria asked.

"Of course." I handed them each a menu. "The specials today honor the music festival. The word *bluegrass* means a certain kind of grass, but now it's also a style of music. Both originated in Kentucky, the state to our south."

"The bluegrass state," Roberto said. "I knew this." He followed with an explanation for Maria, who was looking a bit lost.

"Anyway, fried apples are a specialty of Kentucky, and country ham is big there, too, so we're offering both as specials today." I pointed to the Specials board. "I'll get your coffee."

I was waylaid by two sets of diners, one wanting coffee refills and another customer sending back her omelet, claiming the eggs weren't done. I whispered to Danna, "Cook the life out of it this time."

She raised one eyebrow and slapped the omelet back on the griddle. "Nice and dry, coming right up."

Wanda had pulled up a chair at my father's table by the time I got back. I wasn't sure I liked the look of this. The new deputy sheriff had her trusty notebook and pencil out again. A frown pulled on my father's face.

"Did you contact Pia Bianchi before you arrived in Indiana?" Wanda asked him.

"No," Roberto answered. "I haven't seen her in many years, I told you."

"What about you, ma'am?" Wanda spoke loud and slow.

Seriously? Maria wasn't deaf. She just couldn't speak English very well.

"No, I don't," Maria said, her luminous brown eyes wide.

"You don't what?" Wanda scrunched up her nose.

"I don't talk to her."

"Did you visit her here in Brown County?" Wanda pressed my stepmother.

"No. I say no!"

"Hang on a sec, Wanda," I demanded. "What's going on here?"

"We have intel that your visitors have known Pia Bianchi her whole life. Only makes sense they paid her a visit once they entered the country."

Intel. As if. "Can I have a word with you, please?" I beckoned to Wanda. This was going too far.

Wanda reluctantly stood. "Excuse me, folks." She followed me back to the country store side of the space, where it was quiet and no curious ears would hear.

"What the heck are you doing, grilling my guests when they're ready to eat breakfast?" I folded my arms. "What's this so-called intel you mentioned?"

"When Buck interviewed your father, he learned he and his wife knew the victim. My boss wanted me to follow up." She lifted her chin.

"I told Buck to talk to Roberto. But it was because

they'd seen Pia from a distance the night before she was killed. I thought whatever they saw might be important. Not because I thought he killed Pia!"

"I'm only doing my job, Robbie."

"And I'm only doing mine. I'll thank you to not upset my visiting parents. Let them have their breakfast in peace. Make an appointment and come back if you want, but leave them alone for now. Agreed?"

Wanda tapped her leg with her hand and inspected the far wall from where she stood. Avoiding my gaze, no doubt. Finally she nodded. "Have it your way. But next time we might need him to come down to the station for his interview. Just saying." She stumped back to her table, threw a few bills on it to punctuate her threat, and left, tugging her Smokey Bear hat firmly onto her head as she went.

I checked in with Roberto and Maria. "I hope Wanda didn't upset you." I gazed from one to the other. "She shouldn't have questioned you here, while you were eating."

My father stroked his wife's hand. "She had a small bad experience with *polizia* some years ago. She doesn't like them."

Maria nodded.

"I'm really sorry," I said, then mustered a smile. "What would you like to eat this morning?"

Chapter Nineteen

The bell on the door didn't stop jangling for the next half hour. Every table was full, and three parties milled among the cookware shelves waiting for seats to free up. I didn't have a second to muse over Wanda's questioning, but a little nag at the back of my brain remembered Maria's reaction and what Roberto had said of her past.

Adele followed a group of six diners into the store. With my arms full of empty dishes, it was all I could do to give a little raised-chin smile. Roberto spied Adele and pointed to the empty chair at their table. He'd met her when we'd all had dinner together on Monday. I'd been pretty sure the Italians would like Adele and Samuel, and vice versa, and I wasn't disappointed.

Turner hurried in next, a harried look on his face. "Sorry I'm late, Robbie. There was a tie-up on a small road near my house and they detoured us all the way around by the state park. It took forever." His scent this morning was of fresh air and soap.

I glanced at the wall clock. "It's only eight-fifteen.

Don't worry. You're not very late. But I'm glad to see you." It worked well for Danna to come in at six-thirty, and then to have Turner's help once things got busy. "Check with Danna and see if she wants a break at the grill, okay?" I deposited my armful of dishes at the sink and headed over to say hello to Adele.

"Good morning, Roberta." My aunt beamed. "Sure as heck smells good in here."

I sniffed. It absolutely did. The sweetness of apples and syrup mingled in the air with the savory of sausages and bacon and the richness of dark-roast coffee brewing. The irresistible aroma made my stomach growl right then and there.

Roberto laughed out loud. "When the stomach says such a thing, you need to eat, my daughter."

I had grabbed a biscuit to go with my sausage before we opened, but apparently it wasn't enough. "I'll eat when things slow down in an hour or two." *If* they slowed down.

"We was talking about their schedule today," Adele said.

"She invited us to her farm for lunch," Roberto added. "To see the sheeps."

"Good," I said. "Perfect. And it's such a pretty drive out there." I peered out the window to see sun reflecting off a parked car's windshield. "Looks like a nice day for it, too."

"I'll show 'em the beasts and my garden and all. And get to know each other better." Adele patted Maria's hand. She pointed to herself, then to my stepmother. "Friends, you and me."

Maria smiled and nodded. "Friends."

"Now, can I get me one of them Kentucky omelets, a dish of the apples, and a side of biscuits and gravy?" Adele asked. "I'm a hungry old lady this morning."

I laughed. "Coming right up." I jotted down her order and delivered it to a newly aproned Turner, who had taken over cooking for Danna.

I busied myself asking folks if I could get them anything else, handing out checks, taking money, while Danna cleared and cleaned tables. I told the folks who had been waiting the longest they could be seated. Chase Broward trotted down from upstairs.

"I'm sorry, we're pretty busy right now," I told him. "You'll have to wait ten, maybe twenty minutes for a table to open up." I'd told him and my other B&B guests this kind of situation might arise, that breakfast was first come, first served.

He frowned, crossing his arms on his chest.

"I can get you coffee while you wait, though."

At that, his expression lightened. "Thank you. Coffee will help."

When I returned with his mug of java, though, he wasn't where I'd left him. I scanned the room. *Aha.* I grabbed the coffeepot and carried it and his mug to Roberto and Maria's table where Chase had taken the fourth seat.

After I handed him his coffee and poured Adele's, I said, "This is my aunt, Adele Jordan."

"Hush, now, Robbie," Adele said. "I've knowed Broward here for a coon's age."

"Yes, indeed," Chase said, but he didn't look as slick, as well put-together this morning as he had in previous days. His hand shook enough to make little waves of coffee when he picked up the mug, and he didn't meet Adele's gaze.

Was he nervous for some reason? Hungover? Or maybe he hadn't slept well.

"Do you play again today?" Roberto asked him.

"Yes, later this afternoon. I have a business meeting this morning."

"Are you ready to order?" I asked Chase. "Or should I give you a minute?"

He checked the Specials board, then glanced down at the paper menu, which doubled as place mat. "I'll have the granola and yogurt, please, with a dish of fresh fruit.

I always provided a healthy option, and judging from Chase's trim build, he must opt for it regularly, whether here or at home.

"How's your lovely wife, Chase?" Adele asked as I prepared to leave the group. She set her elbow on her table and rested her chin on her fist. "She hasn't been back to wood-carving club in a month of Sundays."

"No." Chase cleared his throat, his mouth looking like he had tasted spoiled milk. "She still keeps her tools sharp, plays around with different projects."

"Hmm." Adele still gazed at him intently. "You go ahead and tell her I said howdy, all right? She's got spunk, your wife does."

"What's wood-carving club?" I asked my aunt.

"Some of us ladies took a class together a long time ago, got along super," Adele replied. "We decided to start a club so's we could still visit. The plan was for us all to set around and carve stuff, but mostly we snack and gossip. That's the best part."

"Sounds fun." I headed back to the stove, glad he hadn't mentioned the missing card in his room doorway. I also mused on a philanderer's wife owning small very sharp tools, and what else Adele might know about Chase, his wife, and his life.

Chapter Twenty

By a few minutes past eleven the morning rush was over and we were in our usual mid-morning lull. Before she'd left, Adele had moseyed over to me and murmured, "Was it only me, or was Broward more nervous than a long-tailed cat in a room full of rocking chairs?"

"I don't know, Adele. Maybe he didn't get enough sleep," I'd replied.

"Huh. Could be."

Now Danna sat rolling more silverware in the blue cloth napkins we used, and Turner was flipping a few pancakes for his break meal. Feeding my employees was one of their benefits, and the least I could do, really, after running them ragged all morning. I'd finished an omelet—Danna had been right, the contents of the Bluegrass made a great combination—and was munching on a slightly over-crisp piece of bacon when the bell on the door jangled.

Glen Berry ambled in, followed by three other businessmen in town.

"Hey, Robbie," Glen called, lifting a hand in

greeting. His light blue button-down was neatly pressed, with the sleeves rolled up onto his forearms.

I swallowed down the last of the bacon and stood to meet them. "You all here for breakfast, lunch, or both?" Technically I didn't offer lunch until 11:30, but we were almost there. I wasn't going to nitpick it.

"You know Don O'Neill, I think," Glen said.

I nodded and smiled at Abe's older brother, who owned the local hardware store. Don always carried a hint of worry in his face, but I knew he had a good heart.

Glen introduced the other two men. "We wondered if we could reserve a table for every Thursday at, say, eleven-thirty? We're all in business for ourselves and decided it would be good to meet regularly."

Wasn't businesspeople meeting up what the Chamber of Commerce was for? *Whatever.* I was happy to feed them and take their money. "Of course you can, and I thank you for choosing Pans 'N Pancakes for your meeting. Eleven-thirty is a good idea, too, before we get real busy."

Glen glanced at the Specials board, where I'd written Sugar Cream Pie after the breakfast rush was over. He gave a long whistle. "I haven't had me a piece of sugar cream pie in years. I think I've died and gone to my heavenly reward." He rubbed his hands together.

I smiled. "I hope you like it. I used my friend Jane's tried-and-true recipe."

"How have you been, Robbie?" Don asked as I led them toward a four-top at the back.

"I'm good, thanks. Did you hear my father is here visiting?"

Don went pale. *Shoot.* I'd forgotten he'd had a role in the reason my father had to leave the country before his fellowship was over. A role in the reason Roberto had been hospitalized. My father hadn't mentioned Don since he'd been here.

Don paused, gripping the back of a chair.

"Take the square table over there," I said to Glen, pointing at the four-top I had in mind for their meeting. "I'll be with you in a second." I turned to Don. "I'm sorry, Don. It totally slipped my mind that you, um, knew him."

"Have you talked about what . . . what happened?" he whispered, rubbing his head and disturbing his carefully arranged but wispy comb-over.

I shook my head. "No. He hasn't mentioned it." Roberto and I had hashed over the past when I visited him in Italy after Christmas but so far not during this visit. "He's out today, won't be back until afternoon. I truly don't believe he's angry. It was almost three decades ago, after all. But if he does bring you up in conversation, are you willing to meet with him?"

He swallowed hard, some of the color coming back into his face. "I guess. But I'd rather not."

I smiled sympathetically at him. "Go sit down and have your meeting. I doubt you'll run into Roberto. They're leaving tomorrow, anyway."

Don rejoined his group, but he glanced at the door every few minutes as if afraid Roberto would walk in.

Instead, it was Buck who pushed through the door twenty minutes later, with Wanda close behind, both in uniform. Buck's expression was somber as he ambled toward me in front of the cookware shelves, where I had shown a customer the Dover rotary beaters.

"Can we have a word, Robbie?" Buck murmured, surveying the restaurant. When his gaze lit on Glen and his group, Buck pressed his lips together and gave a little shake of his head.

"Of course. What's up?" I gestured for him and Wanda to move down to the end of the area so the shopper wouldn't overhear.

Buck turned his back on the hungry diners, on Danna at the stove, on Turner taking orders.

Wanda began. "We got us another suspicious death this morning."

I stopped smiling. "Another murder?" I whispered.

"Pretty much, from the looks of it," Buck chimed in. "It was on unincorporated county land, but real close to the South Lick line, so I got called in."

"What happened?" I asked, looking from him to Wanda and back. "And how do you know it was murder?"

"When a couple out for their morning walk finds a body by the side of Scarce O' Fat Ridge Road," Buck lowered his voice even further, "and it's got a dang wahr around its—well, *her*—neck, you might as well call it a homicide right from the get-go."

Wahr. In Buck-speak, that would be a *wire*. That must have been the incident Turner had had to detour around. I was almost afraid to ask who *her* was, but I was getting a bad feeling about this. About why Buck had come here in the middle of an investigation. About the look he'd given Glen Berry.

"Was it Sue?" I whispered.

All Wanda had to do was nod once. I inhaled

sharply, bringing my hand to my mouth. Sue. Perky sweet Sue. Mother, grandmother, wife. Sister probably, too, and well-loved in the community. My eyes filled with tears at the unfairness, the injustice of it all. And then . . . "Do you think it's the same person who—"

"Killed Pia?" Wanda broke in. "'Course we don't know yet, but it's a possibility. Maybe Ms. Berry was going around asking too many questions and poof, she meets the same fate." In a totally uncharacteristic gesture, Wanda patted my upper arm. "I'm sorry. You musta been friends with the deceased."

"I didn't know her well, but she and Glen are, were, regulars in here. And then there was the business last year with Erica and all. I liked Sue a lot. She didn't deserve to die." I wiped my eyes with my sleeve as Buck's gaze returned to Glen. I thought for a second more. "Wait. You said the same fate. Do you mean the string around Sue's neck was also a banjo string?" *Garroted.*

"I am sorry to say the answer is yes." Buck sighed. "Might coulda been done by Ms. Bianchi's killer. Or maybe it was one of them copycat murders."

My heart sank. Another murder. The same method. This was terrible news any way you looked at it. "What does copycat mean?" I asked.

"A different bad guy uses the same murder method to try and throw further suspicion on the first killer," Wanda explained.

I nodded. It was a clever thing to do, I supposed. Horrid, evil, despicable—but clever.

Buck cleared his throat. "Right now I have to inform the husband. Not my favorite part of the job,

I'll tell you." He looked at me again. "When'd he get here today, by the way?"

"I'd say it was ten after eleven." Of course Glen would be one of the first suspects. But why would he have killed his wife, who by all public appearances, he seemed to adore? Except, what had he told me? His 1950s-throwback remark? Something about how he couldn't understand why she needed to take a job at all. I imagined most, if not all, marriages had hidden private conflicts. "He asked if he and his friends could reserve a weekly lunch table to talk business."

Wanda hauled out her little notebook and pencil once again and jotted something down. I watched as she and Buck made their way to Glen's table, hats in hand. I watched as Buck leaned over and murmured to Glen, beckoning for him stand. As Glen spread his hands, palms up, in a classic *But why?* gesture. As Buck finally delivered the news right there at the table.

And I watched as Glen leapt to his feet, his face a mask of horror.

Chapter Twenty-one

I hurried up to Wanda as she escorted a slump-shouldered Glen toward the door. I didn't know if she was taking him on the thankless journey to formally identify the body or into an interview room for questioning. Maybe both, in that order. I didn't envy Wanda the task, nor Glen, even more, for what lay ahead. Don had stood, as if wanting to accompany his friend, but Buck had waved him into his seat again.

"I'm so, so sorry, Glen." I laid my hand on his shoulder, my eyes moist anew. He wouldn't be enjoying a piece of sugar cream pie after all.

He blinked as if he'd forgotten where he was. "I do appreciate it, Robbie. Truly I do." His neatly shorn hair, dark brown interlaced with silver, was mussed, like he'd run a hand through it without smoothing it down afterward. His face was ashen.

If Glen had killed Sue and then calmly gathered his colleagues and come in for their first lunch meeting, he was an accomplished actor.

Wanda gestured toward the door. "Mr. Berry?"

He followed her, shaking his head and muttering, "My Susie. My sweet Sue."

I turned to see everyone in the restaurant watching. *Oh, boy.* I cleared my throat. "Everybody? The wife of one of my customers was in a serious accident. These officers came to tell Mr. Berry. That's it. Please don't worry."

Next I approached Turner and Danna. "Glen's received some bad news,"

"Was it Ms. Berry who was hurt?" Danna asked, her eyes wide.

I nodded and made sure my voice was barely above a whisper when I replied. "She was found killed exactly like Pia Bianchi was, is what Buck said."

"The poor thing," Danna said.

Turner swore softly. "That must have been the slowdown this morning."

"I think so," I said. "Until the news goes public, if any customers ask you, please simply say she was in an accident and that's all you know. We wouldn't want the word spreading to her daughter Paula before she hears it from her dad."

"You got it," Danna said.

"No probs," Turner agreed.

I carried Buck's full lunch order over to him twenty minutes later. Double cheeseburger, chips, and my secret-ingredient coleslaw.

"Thank you kindly, Robbie," Buck said, looking up from the phone he'd been jabbing at with one bony forefinger. "Can I get me a double serving of sugar cream pie, too, when you get a minute, please?"

"Of course."

"If I loved sugar cream pie any more, I'd have to get a divorce."

I snorted. "I wouldn't advise it." I knew how fond he was of his wife.

"Sorry for the disturbance," Buck said.

Word travels fast in a small town, and the restaurant was buzzing with customers leaning toward one another, talking about the accident, about Sue, about the grieving widower. I thought I'd caught the word *murder* floating on the airwaves more than once, too. The remaining three businessmen at Glen's table huddled talking.

"You did what you had to do." I tilted my head. "How did you know Glen was here?"

"He left word with one of his staff." Buck took a huge bite of his hamburger, leaving ketchup drizzling down his fingers.

"I'm so sad for Sue, and puzzled," I said. "Who in the world would want to kill her? She's one of the sweetest people in South Lick."

I was grateful Buck swallowed his mouthful before answering me.

"Search me. We know she'd had herself an issue with the first victim. Maybe Ms. Berry got a little too close to the murderer."

I studied him. "You guys questioned Sue. She could still be Pia's killer and somebody else murdered her. Right?" I added when his expression turned skeptical.

"Might coulda happened that way. But rule number one is the old Keep it Simple. Don't help none to fabricate a second killer when the first coulda done both."

"Except you're the one who mentioned a copycat murder," I pointed out.

"That I did. It could be a copycat."

"And Detective Henderson isn't any closer to finding Pia's murderer?"

"You'd have to ask her, Robbie. It ain't my news to share." He pointed his fork at me to reinforce the statement.

"Why do I get the feeling the detective wouldn't share with me, either?"

Buck snorted before taking another impossibly large bite of burger. "You could be right," he mumbled through his food. "Matter of fact, I think you just won the jackpot."

A customer across the room waved his hand at me. I left Buck's table and headed toward the diner, but my brain was at the side of a rural road. A rural road and a finished life.

Chapter Twenty-two

As I turned the sign on the door to CLOSED, wishing I were outside on this lovely pre-summer day, a tinted-window, black SUV drove up and parked. The vehicle featured the star-shaped Sheriff's Department logo on the door, and sure enough, Detective Henderson climbed out. I waved and waited on the porch for her.

"I've been having some difficulty connecting with several of your guests," she said once she'd reached my side and we'd exchanged greetings.

"Two of them are inside having lunch," I offered. Ed and Beth, the fiddler and the clogger, had once again emerged to eat at the last minute before I closed.

A silver sedan pulled up next to the SUV. "And there's my father's rental car," I added, pointing. "They've been at my Aunt Adele's farm since morning. Cell reception can get a little sketchy out there." Adele had hung on to her landline for exactly that reason.

"Excellent," the detective said. "Thank you."

"I'll introduce you." After Roberto and Maria came up the steps, I made the introductions. Maria once again paled at the sight of a uniform. Had she been in trouble with the cops in the past? Roberto had mentioned the *polizia*. I hoped I could squeeze in a moment alone with him to ask what had happened.

"I'd like to ask you each a few questions, if you don't mind. Separately." Henderson removed her hat.

"My wife, her English is not good," Roberto said. "I will interpret for you."

Henderson pressed her lips together, but nodded. "Ms. Jordan, is there a quiet corner inside we can use?"

"Sure. Come on in. The only customers left are the B&B guests and one other table." I held the door open. Once inside I said, "Why don't you sit in my office corner there." I pointed to the desk. The light buzz of conversation in the room stilled at the sight of a uniform, and the contrast between the fresh air outside and the aromas of grilled beef and ham inside made the food scents that much stronger. In a good way.

"Mr. and Ms. Fracasso, if you don't mind?" The detective gestured toward the corner.

Roberto took Maria's elbow and murmured to her in Italian as they went.

Henderson focused on Danna before looking at me. "I'd like to tell your other guests of my intentions. And I'll need to speak to Ms. Beedle while I'm here."

Danna wasn't going to enjoy that any more than the rest of them, but I said, "Follow me." I led the detective to where Ed and Beth were eating—her a cheeseburger and him a Bluegrass omelet—and introduced them.

Beth's eyes widened at the detective.

"I need to interview both of you while I am here," Henderson told them. "It's regarding this week's homicides."

Beth flinched as if she'd been struck. Maybe it was the effect of the word *homicide*, one most of us heard only on television or in the movies.

"We don't know anything about those deaths," Ed said.

"I understand you are in town for the music festival in Beanblossom?" Henderson looked from Ed to Beth, who didn't meet her gaze, and back.

"Yes," Ed said.

"We didn't do anything," Beth protested. "We don't know those people!"

The detective was unfazed. "I have questions for both of you separately. I'll be with you shortly. Please don't leave the premises until we have finished."

"Ohh-kay," Ed said. He patted Beth's hand, murmuring, "It's fine, babe."

Beth didn't look like it was fine, and snatched her hand away as if it wasn't fine to call her *babe*, either.

Henderson walked briskly toward Roberto and Maria.

"Some B&B," Beth muttered. "We come to play music, rent a room, mind our own business, and the cops want to grill us."

I decided to ignore what she'd said. As if the B&B and the murders had any connection. At least, I hoped they didn't. I realized I'd protected Roberto and Maria from being questioned during their meal earlier, but I wasn't doing the same for these guests. I chalked it up to the difference between family and paying guests, or maybe it was the difference between Wanda and the more professional Detective Henderson.

I headed for the stove, which Danna was cleaning quietly while appearing to listen as hard as she could. By prearrangement, Turner had left at one o'clock for a doctor's appointment. He suffered badly from seasonal pollens and molds and had a standing appointment with an allergist.

"What was that all about?" Danna asked. "And who's the lady with the braid, other than some kind of police?"

I'd opened my mouth to answer when one of the local ladies at the four-top raised a finger, catching my eye. "Tell you in a minute," I said to Danna.

After their check was delivered, money was exchanged, and thanks were expressed all around, the ladies headed for the exit. I glanced over at where the detective was seated across from my father and his wife. Maria shook her head vehemently and spoke to Roberto, hands flying as she punctuated her words. I returned to Danna.

"Her name is Anne Henderson."

Danna narrowed her eyes. "I feel like I've seen her before. Does she ever eat in the restaurant?"

"I haven't seen her here. She's the sheriff's detective heading up the investigations into Pia's and Sue's murders."

"That's it." Danna snapped her fingers. "She came

into the high school years ago and warned us against drugs and alcohol. I knew she looked familiar."

"She apparently has questions for everybody in the room right now, including you and me."

"Wonderful. About Isaac's 'whereabouts,' I'm sure." She surrounded the word with finger quotes as the side of her mouth pulled down. "Whatevs." Danna shook her head like she was shaking water out of her dreadlocks after a swim in Lake Lemon.

"Were you at Isaac's place last night?" I asked as I rinsed dishes and loaded them into the dishwasher.

"No. He said he had to go see his dad."

"Where does his father live?"

Danna tilted her head and gazed at me. "He's in a, like, halfway house in Nashville. He got out of prison a month ago on early release, so he has to live in this place and stay out of trouble for a year. But they're helping him get a job and stuff. It could be a lot worse. Didn't I tell you?"

In prison? Did Anne Henderson know this? She must. Or maybe not. "No, you didn't tell me. Can I ask, what was he incarcerated for?"

"It ended up being a stupid reason," Danna went on. "He helped a guy rob a music store. All Isaac's dad did was watch the exit so the other dude could rip off the expensive guitars and all. But they were both convicted of the crime." She shrugged. "Isaac would never do something like that."

Burgle a music store. Stick a few packs of banjo strings in your pocket? Leave them at your son's house? That, added to Pia not paying Isaac what she owed for his work? No wonder the police were interested in Danna's guy. Who, as far as I knew, had zero alibi for the time of Sue's death or for Pia's, depending on if he'd been lying about the body being cold.

At a string of upset Italian words, I turned toward my desk. Maria stood, threw her dark hair back, and stalked to the stairs leading up to the rooms. She tossed a hand in the air in what was almost a carica-ture of an Italian gesture, uttered something, and stepped heavily on each tread, slamming the door at the top.

I returned my gaze to Roberto and the detective. My father sat, arms on his knees, head bowed, while Henderson's erect posture made it look like she was waiting for him to speak. Christ on a cracker, as Adele would say. What just happened?

Chapter Twenty-three

Roberto stood twenty minutes later and came over to the old-fashioned cash register we used, where I was counting the till for the day.

"Are you okay?" I asked.

"I am fine." He blew out a breath. "The detective, she wants to know everything. What did I hear, what did I see." He tossed a hand in the air. "So I tell her. It's no problem for me. I am not a criminal. As my wife is not, also."

Detective Henderson approached Ed and Beth, the only diners left in the restaurant. Their table wasn't far from where Roberto and I stood.

"Ms. Ferguson, if you don't mind?" The detective gestured toward the desk.

I wasn't sure I liked her using my restaurant as an interview room. But if doing so helped solve this case sooner, I wasn't going to complain. Danna followed the action while she scrubbed the grill.

Beth stood. "I really don't see why this is necessary. I don't have anything to tell you."

"Then I'm sure my interview won't take much

more of your time." Henderson's tone was level and brooked no argument.

Beth swore, but stomped over to the office area and stood, arms folded. Henderson followed her. If Beth didn't tell the detective she'd argued with Sue, I was going to have to. Meanwhile Ed sank his forehead into his hand.

"Excuse me a minute," I murmured to my father, shoving the cash drawer shut. I couldn't count money with all this going on. "I'll be right back." He nodded and I headed toward Ed. "Are you okay?" I asked him.

He gazed up at me. "I'm sorry for this mess. She's prone to . . ." His voice trailed off.

Throwing fits? Apparently.

"I mean, she doesn't like the cops. Any of them." He pushed the remnant of his meal—a morsel of ham—around the plate with his fork.

I waited, but he didn't offer any clarification. "Too bad. The police officers I've met are pretty good folks. Did she have a bad experience in her past or something?"

"Sort of." He gazed over toward where Henderson had managed to convince Beth to sit. "She had to serve time on probation a few years ago. They said she was selling drugs, which is ridiculous. All she did was split a bag of weed with a friend of hers. But the friend turned her in to the cops to avoid being charged herself."

"Ouch."

"No effing kidding. It totally derailed her life, too. Beth was ready to start grad school at IU. She'd been dancing her whole life, and was going back to get a

MFA. But when she was arrested the department withdrew her fellowship. It really sucked."

I had a flash of an idea. "Did either of you know Pia Bianchi?" Earlier I thought Beth had said they hadn't, but maybe she'd been lying.

He looked straight at me. "Yes. She was the friend who ratted on Beth."

Whoa. Flash confirmed. "She was?" Talk about a motive for murder. I glanced at the detective. She and Beth were talking but Henderson was keeping her voice too soft for me to hear. "Will Beth admit to it?"

Ed looked sad. "I don't think she'll need to. I'm sure they already know."

Plus Beth had argued with Sue Tuesday night. "This is going to sound funny, but was Beth upstairs with you all night Tuesday?"

He shook his head slowly, watching Beth and Henderson. "She's a runner. She likes going out on long runs to see the sun rise. Me, I have a bum knee, so I can't go with her."

A long run. How long a run? The Beanblossom covered bridge was only three or four miles from here, as was Scarce O' Fat Ridge Road. Beth could have slipped out the upstairs egress without anyone noticing. Would she have arranged to meet Pia at the bridge, coolly choked her with a banjo string around sunrise, and run back? I imagined Henderson was asking Beth the very same questions.

"Did she go for a run yesterday early morning? Or this morning?" I asked.

"Yeah." His already deep voice turned gravelly, trailing out the vowel until it became inaudible.

Did Detective Henderson have any evidence Beth had been at either murder site? I wouldn't interrogate Ed any further. He'd get plenty of questioning from the detective. I almost said something comforting, but I refrained. If his girlfriend was going to be arrested for murder, not a word I could utter would offer any real comfort and would only ring hollow.

"I have to get back to my father. You make sure to let me know if there's anything you need, okay?" Like the name of a good lawyer, maybe.

"Thanks, Robbie. This sure isn't how I expected this week to go. It was supposed to be a fun getaway for the two of us.

"Don't you live in Bloomington?" I asked.

"Yes, but we both share houses with other people. I wanted this week to be special. A romantic bed-and-breakfast, great scenery, a week full of the music we love. Clogging for her, fiddling for me. We were trying to sort of patch up a rough spot in our relationship, frankly. Instead, the past reared its ugly head." He set his chin on both fists and blew out a breath of frustration between his lips.

"I'm sorry to hear that."

Ed gave me a wan smile. "I shouldn't have unloaded my problems on you. Go talk to your dad. He looks like a nice guy."

I smiled back. "He is."

By now my father was elbow deep in sudsy water. When I neared him, I admonished him. "*Babbo*, you don't have to wash dishes." The affectionate Italian for "father" was still unfamiliar on my tongue.

His smile could have powered the electricity needs

for all of South Lick. "But of course I help. You have your customers, Miss Danna she works alone, I am sitting there?" He flipped open both hands, Italian style, nailing me with a clump of suds in the eye.

While Danna doubled over laughing, I grabbed my sleeve and wiped my eye.

"*Colpa mia, cara.*" Roberto looked worried. "I am sorry for the . . ." His voice trailed off and he waved his hands again, leaving more suds flying.

I waved down his concerns. "It's okay, really. It's not your fault. It would be even more okay if Danna didn't think it was so funny," I mock scolded her.

I didn't mind being laughed at. Frankly, it was a welcome break from what Ed had told me, and from the ultra-serious conversation going on near my desk. Beth looked as somber and concerned as Ed. I grabbed a damp rag and set to wiping down all the tables, setting them with fresh place mats and silver-ware rolls until I ran out, then sat with the baskets of flatware and a stack of clean napkins to assemble more.

Roberto joined me. "I will help you."

I showed him how to lay a knife, fork, and spoon on the diagonal of a square napkin. He slid the napkin over to me and I did the fold-and-roll maneuver. We assembled in silence for several minutes as Henderson questioned Beth, Danna swept the floors, and Ed perused his phone. With a furrowed brow, he glanced over at Beth every once in a while.

"Roberto," I began in a low voice, abandoning the Italian term for now. "Why does Maria seem to dislike the police so much?"

He let out a sigh. "She has a brother who got in some big trouble. He was doing illegal things. She hated what the police did to him."

I decided not to ask what kind of illegal things, even though I was curious. "But she herself hasn't been arrested or anything?"

"Not since I have known her, no."

Huh. That sounded a little vague. As if he knew she'd done something wrong before they'd met? Like when he was here with my mom, maybe. It couldn't have any bearing on the current crimes. Or at least I hoped not.

"She's probably going to have to talk to the detective at more length at some point," I said.

"I know this. Maria knows this. She is tired and said she must pack our suitcases."

"I hate to think of you both leaving." I gazed at him across the table and ended with the truth. "I want more time with you."

"As do I. So we will make it possible." My father pushed the last loaded napkin over to me. I counted the number of rolls. Nowhere near enough for tomorrow. It was time to start a load of store laundry.

Before I could grab the hamper of soiled linens, Beth stood abruptly.

"I can't keep repeating myself," she spit out, word by word. "I didn't murder anybody. Yesterday I went for an early run. Today I went for an early run. Isn't it your job to find someone who saw me killing those women? I thought I didn't have to prove myself innocent!" She stormed out the door.

Chapter Twenty-four

I listened to the cowbell on the door continue to jangle after Beth slammed it behind her. If Buck was here, he'd say she was madder than a hen on a June bug in summer. Ed jumped up and set the bell to jangling again as he followed her.

"Mr. Molina?" Detective Henderson called after him, but it was too late. "Okay," she said, drawing out the word as if his departure wasn't actually okay. She cleared her throat. "Ms. Beedle, might you have a few minutes to spare?" She gave Danna a polite smile.

Danna glanced at me.

"You've done enough for today. Permission granted."

Danna dried her hands before joining Henderson at the desk. Roberto stood.

"I go to rest now," he said. "And perhaps to smooth my wife."

I figured he meant *soothe*, but I didn't correct him.

Smoothing was good, too. "See you back down here at six, all right?"

"*Alle sei in punto.*" He headed for the stairs, ascending with a slow heavy step.

My phone buzzed in my back pocket. When I checked, it was a calendar reminder to put in the order for the weekend. I swore to myself. The end of the afternoon would squeak in for delivery tomorrow. Four o'clock was their cutoff, and I had exactly ten minutes. I hurried over to the desk, where Danna already looked exasperated with the detective's questions.

"I told you. I left Isaac's house before six Wednesday morning. I had to zip home before I came to work. He was already out with the dog. What more can I say?" Danna flipped her palms open to the sides.

"Excuse me," I said to Henderson. "I need to grab something."

She scooted back in the office chair so I could open the top drawer and extract my tablet. I carried it into the walk-in cooler and pulled up the ordering app. Turner wanted to make an Asian noodle salad, and luckily buckwheat soba noodles were available. I really should stock soba regularly so I could offer a gluten-free option for those with sensitivities. I added sugar snap peas, red peppers, and carrots, plus a bottle of rice wine vinegar. Soon I'd be able to get almost all my produce at the Nashville farmers' market. I checked on our other staples and added butter, milk, bacon, and eggs to the order. I included sliced turkey meat for the Hot Brown sandwiches, plus a few other odds and ends, and hit SEND. *Whew.*

Shivering from the low temperature of the walk-in, I clicked the heavy door shut behind me. Danna and Henderson were still in conversation, or in interview mode, more accurately. The detective never seemed to lose her cool. Was it part of her training or in her nature to be calm and centered even when digging into the depths of people's motivations and fears? I knew from personal experience investigating a homicide could be very, very dangerous, and it wasn't even my job. I admired those who were brave enough to make it their profession.

Once again I hoisted the full hamper and aimed myself for my apartment, where I'd installed the washer and dryer. I shot a glance at Danna and caught her attention. "I'll be right back," I called. She gave me a thumbs-up in return.

The door to my private quarters was at the back of the store. I fumbled in my pocket for the key, trying to hang on to the heavy hamper.

"Can I help you?" a man's voice asked from directly behind me.

It startled me so much I dropped the hamper on my foot. My key fell into the open top. An expletive slipped out of my mouth before I could catch it. I whirled to see Chase backing up a step. Where had he come from? Not through the front door. He must have gone up the outdoor stairs and into the rental space before coming down here. The second egress for the B&B rooms, required by the building code, was a staircase outside the eastern side of the building.

"Sorry, didn't mean to startle you," he said.

Over his shoulder I saw Henderson start to stand. "It's all right," I called over to her. "I'm fine." To Chase I added, "I thought you were going to be out all day."

"I forgot something in my room." His dark eyes regarded me.

I didn't know quite why, but I was suddenly grateful an officer of the law and a tall strong young woman kept me company right now. "I see. Well, if you'll excuse me, I'm still on the clock." I righted the hamper, scooping back in the dirty towels and napkins that had fallen when I dropped the hamper. I swore again, silently this time. My key was in there somewhere, too.

Chase cleared his throat. "I know you're closed, but I wondered if I could make myself a quick sandwich or something to tide me over."

Giving bed-and-breakfast guests afternoon snacks hadn't been in my mission statement, but then again, the customer is always right. "Sure. I'll get you set up."

He followed me to the cook station. I pulled out a clean plate, cutting board, and knife. I pointed to the bread. "Help yourself. You can find cheese in the small fridge underneath the counter, and the pickle jar is right behind you."

"I appreciate it, Robbie."

"No worries." I was a bit worried, however, as I returned to my long-suffering hamper and dug into it until I felt the metal key. I knew Chase had said he had playing gigs lined up for the afternoon. Three o'clock was eminently qualified to be called afternoon. So what was he doing here?

Chapter Twenty-five

I sat in my apartment, alone at last, at five o'clock. We had a dinner reservation for six o'clock at Hoosier Hollow—Roberto, Maria, Abe, and me—and I'd already finished the prep for tomorrow morning's breakfast except for the silverware rolls. The laundry was finally in the dryer, and Roberto and Maria were resting upstairs. Danna had gone home after Detective Henderson was through with her, and I could tell my employee wasn't a bit happy over the way the questioning had gone. Henderson had taken the opportunity to shoot some questions at Chase while he was eating his free cheese sandwich. I'd watched out of the corner of my eye as I prepped biscuit dough. Chase hadn't looked particularly pleased with the grilling, either.

I was beat, but my mind was racing from the fullness of the day. I could fix busy-brain syndrome by doing one of two things: go for a strenuous bike ride to clear out my brain or create a crossword puzzle to make sense of what I knew. The first option was out because I didn't have enough time. So I poured a cool IPA, got my graph paper, ruler, and sharp pencil, and sat at the kitchen table with my feet resting on the other chair. Birdy jumped up and curled around my feet for a nap.

"What do I know, Birdman?" I asked him, but he kept his silence. Pia had had tussles of one kind or another with Sue, and with Glen, too. With Chase. With Isaac. Even with Abe. Any of them could have wanted her gone—except Abe, of course. So I started the puzzle with *PIA BIANCHI* across. I intersected *ISAAC* down through the *I* of her first name and *CHASE* going down from the *C* in her last name That led to *SUE*, who of course was dead, too. Glen's name I added ending in the *N* of *BIANCHI*. I used the *B* of the name to print *BEANBLOSSOM* going down. I knew Abe wasn't a suspect, but I added his name off the second *B* in the town's name, anyway.

I sat back and sipped the nicely hoppy ale, which held a hint of grapefruit. The tricky question now was Sue's death. It still hung over my emotions like a thick cold fog. The motivation for killing her either had to come from Pia's murderer or from someone else who wanted her dead. Could it be the apparently grieving Glen? The Glen who wasn't happy with Sue working a job that didn't revolve around him and their home? Of course, if he'd killed Pia, and if Sue had been asking questions regarding the murder, then he'd have double the reason to remove his wife from the scene. But had she been? If Glen was innocent in both killings, he was just a grieving husband. Maybe tomorrow I could find time to take some food over to him.

If Chase was Sue's killer, he would have had to

sneak out this morning without me noticing, go do the deed, sneak back in, and then come down for breakfast. He had looked a bit rattled this morning, not presenting the usual neat and trim front he usually did. B&B parking was on the far side of the store where the outside stairs were, and that side of the store didn't have any windows. So Chase easily could have slipped away early, while I was busy with the noise of frying bacon and greeting customers. But how would he have lured her to wherever it was that he killed her? I flashed on the scene at the music festival when I'd spied the two of them arguing about something. It had been the night after Pia was discovered. Had Sue suspected Chase? I shook my head. I might never know.

I returned to the puzzle. Anne Henderson should be an entry, and her name fit nicely intersecting with *CHASE* at the *A*. How much progress was she making, anyway? I hung *WANDA BIRD* off the first *N* in *HENDERSON*, since they were working together. Were they ferreting out alibis? Had the medical examiner given them a window of time during which Pia had died? Isaac had said her body was cold when he found her. And then there was Sue's time of death. The traffic pileup had been this morning before eight. If Glen had faked his grief, he could also have easily lied about when Sue left home, and how else would the police know? They could ask neighbors if anyone saw her, I supposed.

I hung the word *MURDER* off the final letter of *BEANBLOSSOM*, and crossed the *I* in *BIRD* with *ACCIDENT*. *BANJO STRING* fit down on the final letter of *HENDERSON*,

BUCK worked off the top of *BANJO* and *WEAPON* squeezed in on the end of *STRING*. Clues were what I needed, except adding *CLUES* ending on a *BEANBLOSSOM S* did nothing to bring any to mind. Still, it gave me a place to hang *ALIBI*.

Danna was Isaac's alibi for Pia's death—or was she? Maybe he'd lied that the body had been cold when he found Pia. Maybe he'd met her by arrangement in the bridge, leaving before Danna left for work. He could have waited to use the parson's phone until more time had passed. But if so, killing Pia wasn't a spur-of-the-moment, PTSD flare-up kind of crime. Why would Isaac even have a banjo string on him? I wondered if Danna had stayed at Isaac's last night, too, or if he was without an alibi for Sue's murder, too. Isaac's father had been in prison. Had his criminal behavior rubbed off on his son? I scribed *PRISON* going down off *WEAPON*.

Maybe Sue's killer was none of the people involved in Pia's death. Buck had mentioned a copycat murder. While I chewed over that, I used the first *C* in *ACCIDENT* to add *COPYCAT* to the puzzle. Anybody could get their hands on a banjo string. Sue might have had a long-standing issue with someone over any number of life's problems. Why do people kill? For love, for money, for revenge. And she was such a little woman, almost anybody could have physically killed her. I shivered, picturing the actual act of choking a fellow human being to death. Wouldn't they struggle? Wouldn't it be unbearably awful? What life situation was so terrible someone would take such a final, fatal step?

Buck had said a couple out for a stroll had found Sue's body by the side of Scarce O' Fat Ridge Road. Surely whoever took her there would have left some kind of evidence in his or her car. A hair, a smear of blood, evidence of a struggle, something the police could use. I frowned and tapped my pencil against the puzzle. How would anyone but Glen have convinced Sue to get in a car early in the morning? Glen had an early morning habit of leaving the house. I supposed somebody could have broken into the Berry home and forced Sue out. Or killed her there and then dumped the body? But why, especially if they weren't also Pia's killer?

And then there was Beth. She had a strong motive for murdering Pia. She had argued with Sue. Her long solo run provided means, opportunity. I used the *E* in MURDER to add Beth, and hung RUN off the first *R*. Beth had been incensed at Henderson's implication she might have killed Pia. But did she protest so much because she was guilty or innocent? I used the *G* in GLEN to add GUILTY at the top of the puzzle and the *N* of PRISON to write INNOCENT at the bottom, which gave a pleasing symmetry to the grid. *MEANS* also fit nicely crossing the third *N* of INNOCENT. I stared at the puzzle and then wrote GARROTED off the R in BANJO STRING. And because I could, I added SEVENTH using the *N* of RUN and the *H* of BETH, because today was June seventh.

I sat back again. I wasn't sure if this puzzle exercise was helping, after all. Nothing seemed particularly clear, and now my stomach was queasy from imagining the two killings. My only hope was that the sheriff's detective was having better luck with the facts. When my phone buzzed in my back pocket in the middle of my puzzling, I jumped, then extracted it and answered Abe's call.

"Sweetie, I heard about Sue's death," he began. "It's terrible news."

"I know. Buck and Wanda came into the restaurant to tell Glen."

"How did he take it?"

"He seemed very much like a man stricken with grief," I said.

Abe didn't speak for a few seconds. "What do you mean, seemed very much like?" he finally queried.

"I mean, it's possible he was acting sorrowful. You know the police often suspect the spouse first."

"Ugh. Really?"

"Yes. I'm not totally sure why he would kill his own wife or if it had anything to do with Pia's death."

"Wow," Abe said. "A lot to take in. If Glen is innocent, he's going to be a wreck. Losing Sue less than a year after losing his own daughter? And both from murder? It doesn't give you a good feeling about the world, does it?"

"No." I finished the last sip of beer. "So let's ignore the whole thing and head out for a nice meal, shall we?"

"That's the other reason I called. I'm sorry, Robbie, I can't make it after all. Sean's mom's father, my former father-in-law, was taken ill and she had to get down to Evansville. I'm on dad duty."

What a disappointment. I'd been looking forward to having him at my side during dinner at the place where we'd had our first date. "Want to bring Sean, too?"

"That won't work, either. He has a final exam to-morrow to study for, and I agreed to help quiz him. We'll be eating Dad's famous chili and hot dogs instead of gourmet cuisine, I'm afraid."

"Okay. Thanks for letting me know. We'll miss you. I'll miss you."

"I know, and I'm sorry. It's just one of those things. When are the Italians taking off?"

"Tomorrow afternoon. It's been a short visit, but a nice one. Too bad murder had to mess things up."

"Please tell them I said good-bye, then. And I'll take a rain check on dinner."

We said our farewells and disconnected. I wouldn't have my favorite guy next to me tonight. Too bad. Glen would never have Sue by his side again, ever. Whether he preferred it that way or not remained to be seen.

Chapter Twenty-six

Roberto savored a bite of his batter-fried catfish. "Mmm, exactly like I remembered it. Your friend, the chef, she is very talented." He smiled.

"She is," I agreed. We'd been at Hoosier Hollow restaurant for forty-five minutes. Christina had sent out a complimentary appetizer sampler, which we'd leisurely enjoyed with our first round of drinks. The place, open less than a year, was within walking distance of my store, and was thriving, by the looks of it. Every table was full, and I was glad I'd made reservations.

Maria had opted for the chicken in a creamy wine-mushroom sauce over savory grits after my father explained grits were a lot like polenta. "I am sorry, no Abe," she said.

"*Anch'io*," I said, trying out what I thought was Italian for "I am, too."

Maria laughed and nodded.

"*Molto bene*, Roberta," Roberto said.

I took another bite of my Cajun crayfish stew, a delectable thick sauce brimming with crayfish tails,

which thankfully had already been shelled. I inhaled
the flavors of the fishy meat, the rich tomato sauce,
the herbs and peppers and onions all cooked down
together. It was served over white rice and was spicy
enough to suit my California taste buds. A candle
flickered in a jar on the table. The artwork on the
walls, quirky scenes painted in a folk-art style, reflected
summer in Brown County. One had teens cannon-
balling off a huge boulder into a clear lake. Another
showed a busy farmers' market, with an Amish family
selling vegetables and jars of honey, while the painting closest to us featured a canopy of leaves and two
girls fishing next to a red covered bridge. I glanced
at it and then glanced away. Covered bridges weren't
my idea of a good time right now.

"How was your visit to Adele's farm?" I asked. I'd
phoned her to see if she could take Abe's place at
dinner, but she and Samuel had other plans.

"I love the sheeps," Maria said.

"Adele works hard there," Roberto said. "She is
not young. She keeps all those animals and has a big
garden, too."

"I know, but she loves it." I sipped the cool, crisp
pinot gris we'd ordered. "Maybe it keeps her feeling
young to be so active."

My father nodded.

I gazed at him, this man I looked so much like but
knew so little of. "Tell me about your life when you
were growing up. What did you like to do? What
games did you play? What was your favorite food?"
The kinds of things he might have told me as I was
growing up, except we hadn't had the chance.

Roberto laughed. "You know, I was a typical Italian

boy. I played the football—what you call soccer. I went to mass. I ate what my mama served me, except I didn't like olives. Too salty."

I smiled. "I didn't like olives when I was young, either."

"We had lots of talking in my family at the dinner table. Politics, history, everything. So later I was on the *discussione* team, when I was sixteen."

"The discussion team?"

He thought hard. "I think you call it the debate."

My eyes widened. "I was on debate team, too! I loved it."

"But enough about me."

I would never get enough of him, and this trip had been too short, too full of busy. I resolved to make time to go back to Italy before the year was out.

My father lifted his glass. "Here is to you and your business, Robbie, and your happiness."

Maria and I clinked our glasses with him, and I added, "*Buon viaggio* to you both. It's been wonderful to have you here." I had opened my mouth to apologize for the murders happening during their trip, and for not being able to take time off from the store when I saw Don O'Neill approach our table. Roberto had his back to Don.

"Pardon me, folks," Don began. He came a little farther around the table.

Roberto's eyes widened. "I would know that voice anywhere." He squinted at Don. "But you look different, my friend." He stood and extended his hand to Don.

"I have been carrying a heavy burden." Don clasped Roberto's hand with both of his. He exhaled and swallowed hard. "I need to apologize to you. I am sorry. What I did was wrong, cruel, and criminal. I have been repenting all these years. Please forgive me." The last came out as a plea.

Roberto gazed into Don's eyes and clapped his free hand on Don's shoulder. "I do not keep the grudge. I am well, I am happy, I have *famiglia*, and I have found my first daughter. What else could I want? I forgave you many years ago."

With his bowed shoulders and worried eyes, Don truly had looked like he'd been under a load. Now his posture lightened, and he smiled with his entire face. "Thank you, brother. You mean it?"

"*Sì, certo.* Of course I mean it."

"God bless you," Don said. "May we have coffee together while you are here? I could take you to see my parents again, too. They were asking after you."

Why hadn't I thought of that? I liked the senior O'Neills very much, and they would have been happy to see Roberto again.

"But we leave tomorrow, unfortunately," Roberto said. "So coffee in the morning, yes, but you will have to greet your parents for me." He smiled. "This is my wife, Maria."

"So pleased to meet you, ma'am," Don said.

"I also pleased," Maria answered.

"You should all come to visit us in Pisa," Roberto said.

Maria nodded. "Yes, visit."

"Don, can you join us for dinner?" I asked, pointing. "We have an extra seat." If he did, I might be able to swing the conversation around to Glen for a few minutes.

"Thank you, no. I'm working in the store. I saw you folks come in and had to wait for my evening employee to arrive before I came across the street." Don owned the hardware store in town.

I thought maybe he also used the time so he could get his nerve up to face Roberto with his apology.

"Coffee at ten?" he asked Roberto.

"Coffee at ten." My father sat again, but not before embracing Don.

"*Ciao*," Don said, his eyes damp.

"*Ciao, caro*," Maria said. She watched him go and turned to Roberto for a quick exchange in Italian, which ended with her nodding as if she finally understood the details.

"I'm glad he came to speak with you," I said.

"Yes, as I am, also." My father gazed at where Don had gone but perhaps his real gaze was at himself all those years ago, when he and my mother had fallen in love and ended up separated by thousands of miles.

I still hoped to talk with Don about Glen. "I'm sorry." I stood quickly. "I'll be right back." I hurried out the door. Luckily for me, Don was waiting for a line of motorcycles to rumble by before crossing the road.

"Don?" I said, touching his arm.

Startled, he turned to face me. "Oh, Robbie. I am so glad I spoke to my old friend." He was still standing tall, and somehow looked a few years younger.

"Me, too. But I wanted to ask you a question. Did you talk to Glen again today? I wonder how he took the news of Sue's death."

"Glen." Don shook his head. "Can you believe

the police had to question him? In his grief, he was forced to answer questions regarding where he was this morning, had anyone seen him, the works. They have no respect over there in the sheriff's office."

"Did they, um, detain him?" I didn't want to use the word *arrest*, but I also wanted to know where he was.

"No. They let him go home around four, he said. He had to go and tell Paula her mother was dead. I can't even imagine the pain of it. Her with the baby and all."

The motorcycles finished their passage, the last one disappearing around the next corner.

"I'd better get back to the store," Don said.

"Okay. And thanks for being brave enough to apologize. I know it meant a lot to my father."

He smiled sadly. "It was the least I could do, really."

Chapter Twenty-seven

I sat in my restaurant at nine o'clock with Roberto and Maria and covered a yawn with my hand. "Excuse me. It's been a long day."

They'd offered to help make napkin rolls after we'd walked home from Hoosier Hollow, an offer I gladly accepted. I poured us each a small glass of the special limoncello they'd brought me.

"To Robbie," Maria said lifting hers.

We clinked three ways, and I added, "To many more visits in the future," before I sipped.

"Many, many more," Roberto agreed. His phone dinged in his blazer pocket. He drew it out and frowned at what he saw. He swiped and poked and frowned more deeply, then looked up. "Our flight, it's not going tomorrow." He repeated in Italian for Maria.

"It was canceled?" I asked. "Why?"

"They say a *vulcano* in Islanda is active. There is too much, how do you say, *cenere* in the air."

"Ash?" I tilted my head. "That can happen from volcanic eruptions. Where is Islanda?"

"You know, small island country in the north," Roberto said.

"Ah. Iceland. So no flights in Europe? The ash must mess up their engines."

He nodded. "They say maybe the next day we fly, or maybe not." He smiled as he lifted a shoulder and dropped it. "So we stay longer. This is fine with you, my daughter?"

"Of course it is. And I'm glad you can stay." I went into my apartment to grab the hamper of clean laundry and let Birdy come back into the store with me. "Let's pull out the blue napkins." I held one up so Maria could follow what I was saying. "I can fold the rest later."

Maria shook her head. "I fold." She commandeered the laundry basket, sorting through and pulling out all the napkins and laying them flat on the table. Roberto smoothed them as they arrived. Maria cleared the next table over and began to fold the rest of the load, mostly dish towels and aprons. I carried the clean silverware basket from the dishwasher to the table and listened while she and Roberto chatted in Italian for a few minutes. I sat, folding and rolling, letting the melodic language wash over me, not even trying to understand.

What a treat to have another day or two with them. Too bad the murders in the background tainted the visit for all of us, as selfish as it sounded. My overly busy schedule didn't help, either. I could send them off on a junket tomorrow while I worked, if they wanted. They could go west and visit Columbus, Indiana, a town with interesting architecture. Or they could drive south to French Lick or even all the way to Evansville or into Kentucky, for that matter. Pretty countryside surrounded us in all directions this far south in the state. It was quite different from the flat farming terrain of the northern half, where soybeans and corn flourished.

I heard a rapping on the glass in the front door to the store. My father's gaze met mine as a chill ran through me. There was, in fact, still a murderer on the loose in the county. Possibly two. On the other hand, killers don't normally come knocking. I shook off the feeling and headed to the door, flipping on the outside lights when I got there.

Ed stood peering in, with Beth close behind him. I unbolted the door and let them in.

"Sorry about that. We didn't have our key to the upstairs with us," he said.

"Not a problem," I said.

Beth's shoulders drooped and her lips were pressed into a line. I couldn't tell if her expression was serious sad or serious determined.

"Did you come from the festival?" I asked.

Beth nodded slowly. "It wasn't very festive, though. A lot of people seemed to be mourning Sue Berry."

"She did such a good job of keeping things running well," Ed added. "There were definitely some glitches tonight."

"Sue had really found her superpower with the festival job," I said. "It's awful she's gone. Did either of you know her? I mean, before this week?"

Beth's nostrils flared and her serious expression turned to a glare. *Oops.* I might have just poked a hornet's nest.

"No, we didn't know her," Ed hurried to say before

Beth could explode at me. He took Beth's hand. "Come on, hon. Let's get to bed."

I'd be willing to bet one of them was lying about that, and probably both. With Beth's volatile temper, it seemed even the smallest of slights triggered an extreme reaction. What if Beth had a run-in with Sue at some point in the past, and the disagreement about the entrance fee pushed Beth's anger over the edge?

"Good night, then." I watched them trudge up the stairs until they were out of sight. Chase and Beth were both on Detective Henderson's suspect list, or at least her persons-of-interest list, and they were on mine, too. I was surprised I wasn't more freaked out by having a potential killer under my roof, and down the hall from my father, too.

I turned back to Roberto and Maria. A stack of neatly folded clean towels sat next to one of aprons, and the table where I'd sat was now loaded with dozens of napkin rolls. Maria stared at her phone and murmured in Italian to her husband. Roberto glanced up when I joined them.

"Is something wrong?" I asked.

"Maria, she's reading the news from home. Pia's murder is the big story. And the story says we, my wife and I, are involved."

"That's crazy. You're involved because you're staying in the next town from where somebody was killed?" How had the reporter even found out?

"*Colpevole,*" Maria whispered, her face drained of color.

"What?" I asked.

Roberto squeezed Maria's hand. "It says we are guilty."

Chapter Twenty-eight

I yawned as I headed for the coffeepot in the restaurant at six the next morning. It had taken both Roberto and me to talk Maria off the cliff. I didn't understand why an Italian news agency would make such an accusation, or even how they knew my father and his wife were here. Roberto kept stroking Maria's hand and talking calmly to her in Italian, and they finally went up to bed. I'd encouraged them to lock their room door, and I made sure to turn the bolt on the door to my apartment, too.

This business of one, possibly two murderers still not apprehended was getting old, and it made me nervous that I might be harboring one—or both?—of them upstairs. I wondered if providing keys to the second egress had been the smartest idea in the world. On my next day off, I was buying and installing the camera as the detective had recommended to track the comings and goings of my guests. For now good locks were going to have to suffice.

After I started the coffee and lit the oven, I rolled and cut biscuits, and slid the first couple of batches into the oven to bake. The second baking sheet grated on the oven shelf. My eyes flew wide open. I remembered hearing a sound resembling that in the middle of the night. A scraping, almost chipping kind of noise. It had seemed to be part of the dream I was immersed in—until it roused me. I hadn't really awoken enough for the sound to worry me, though, and had sunk back into the odd semi-real world of dreams.

But with a murderer or two at large and me now fully awake, I very much wanted to know what had made the noise. I knew it wasn't a cat noise, and besides, Birdy had been sound asleep on my feet. I walked over to the door to my apartment. It was intact. I hurried through my apartment to the back door.

And sucked in a harsh breath. Scratch marks surrounded the metal plate that held the keyhole and handle to the door. My heart departed to the Arctic. Someone had tried to get to me in the night. Who else besides the killer? Or one of them?

I made myself return to my prep and practiced deep calming breathing. It was still only six-twenty when Danna burst in. Her eyes were wide and her dreds flew every which way.

"What's the matter, Danna? You look like a ghost was chasing you."

"I can't find Isaac."

"What do you mean, you can't find him?"

"He's gone. I couldn't reach him last night. We were supposed to go to the music festival and he never came to get me." The words rushed out of her. "He didn't answer my texts or my e-mails, and didn't pick up when I called. I went over to his place but his truck isn't there!"

"Try to calm down a little, okay? Maybe he got an emergency call and had to leave."

"But he at least would have texted me."

"Where do his parents live? Could he have gone to see them?"

"His dad is in the halfway house."

"Right. I forgot. How about his mom?"

"She lives up in Zionsville, you know, near Indy. I don't know her number or anything," she wailed. "Robbie, what if Isaac was murdered, too?"

My ultracompetent assistant was only twenty, and I knew she'd fallen hard for Isaac. But given what she'd said, that he was a veteran and prone to flashes of temper, it wouldn't surprise me if he'd gone off somewhere to be alone. Or was he trying to escape the police? Maybe Henderson had asked him in for more questioning and he didn't want to go. Because he was guilty, *colpevole*? Or he went and the police had detained him overnight. Wouldn't they have to arrest him to keep him for so long? I knew they had to have evidence to make an arrest. But Isaac murdered, too? That was a possibility I didn't even want to consider.

"Listen, Danna. I need your help this morning, but after Turner comes in, why don't you take a break? Make some calls. See if he's at his mother's place. Or maybe he's at the police station. Let's not jump to another murder so quickly."

She shook her head fast. "But he didn't do anything wrong. I know he didn't."

"It's one possibility." *So was murder.* I was pretty sure

Isaac hadn't come to my door trying to get in, but it was theoretically possible. "Buck usually comes in for breakfast. We can ask him what he knows." I took a deep breath and let it out, modeling for her. "Take a deep breath. Grab an apron. That sign is getting turned to OPEN in half an hour, and we need to be ready." She knew the routine, and I hoped it would steady her to do familiar work in a safe, familiar place.

She accomplished her own deep inhale and exhale. "All right." She dug a purple bandanna out of her bag before she stashed it under the counter and tied the bandanna around her head. "I'm sorry, Robbie. It's so not like him to take off without telling me." She hurried into the walk-in and came out with the tray full of condiment caddies we put on each table.

I beat the wet ingredients into the dry pancake mix and started a dozen sausages on the grill as Danna distributed the caddies.

"By the way, I put the order in yesterday afternoon, but if they don't deliver this morning, we won't be able to do the Hot Brown sandwich or Turner's Asian noodle dish," I said. "My bad."

"We can do them tomorrow, instead. I was thinking to whip up some blueberry muffins this morning. We have frozen berries."

"Great idea." I was glad her distress wasn't dimming her creativity for thinking up specials.

When seven o'clock hit, we were ready, including several dozen fruity muffins in the oven adding the aromatic lure of baked goods to the air. I turned the sign to OPEN and pulled open the door to six customers already waiting on the porch.

"Good morning everyone," I said, smiling my welcoming-proprietor face, no matter what was going on behind it. "Come on in." I stood back to let them enter, then surveyed the day for a minute. The air was already warm and the sky was clear, the sun rising above the green-leafed trees across the road. It was forecast to be a scorcher today, which was unusual for early June. But a hot sunny day was a lot better for festivalgoers than a rainy one. I hoped it would be a good day for Detective Henderson, too. It was time to get the murderer caught and safely behind bars. Unless it was Isaac and he was already there.

Chapter Twenty-nine

By seven-thirty the place was nearly full. I glanced up from the grill as the cowbell jangled again. It was Phil, arms loaded with brownies.

"Bring them on over," I called. I kept working, a stainless turner in each hand so I could flip pancakes, move omelets around, turn sausages, sauté onions and peppers, and accomplish all the other tasks of a short-order cook.

As Phil set the trays on the counter, the delectable aroma of chocolate wafted straight into my brain. "You just baked those? I feel like I've died and gone to heaven."

He laughed. "Yeah, got up early, thought I'd use the time wisely." The smile slid away. "The music department is having a memorial for Pia at the end of the day today. Any chance you want to come?"

"I didn't know her very well. She'd only recently joined my puzzle group. I'll send out a text to the group about the service, though. Where will it be?"

"At four o'clock in Beck Chapel on the IU campus. Afterward a bunch of us are going to eat at DeAngelo's."

"Italian food in memory of an Italian. Good idea."
I flipped four pancakes and laid three pieces of
bacon on the hot grill. "My father and Maria were
supposed to leave this afternoon but their flight got
postponed, so I'm not sure what I'll be doing with
them after I close today."

"I read about the volcanic ash disrupting all kinds
of things."

Danna hurried over with two more orders, slap-
ping the slips on the carousel. "Hey, Phil. You haven't
seen Isaac around town, have you?"

"No. Did you lose him?"

"Kind of. If you spot him, will you text me? And
ask him to call?" She loaded up her arms with two
ready platters.

"Sure. Hope he turns up," Phil added.

"You and me both, dude." Danna carried the
plates to their destination.

"What's up with her?" Phil asked me.

"Isaac stood her up last night. He appears to be incommunicado, and his truck wasn't at his place this
morning. She's worried."

"Do you think he had something to do with Pia's
death?"

"I don't know what to think. I don't know the guy
at all." The cowbell jangled again. "But here's somebody who can at least tell us if Isaac is or isn't at the
police station. Morning, Buck," I called.

Buck ambled over and greeted us. "Going to snag
me a table."

"And you want the usual?" I asked.

"I surely do. I've got a pit the size of the Grand
Canyon in my stomach."

Phil murmured, "For a change."

"Ain't that the way of it?" Buck said.

I spied Danna watching us. "Buck, before you sit down, would you happen to know if Detective Henderson has Isaac in custody?"

"The Rowling fella?"

"Yes," I said.

"Hey Robbie, I have to split," Phil said. "Maybe I'll see you this afternoon."

"I'll try."

"See ya, Buck."

Buck waved his hand. "Welp, I'm not sure I know the answer to your question. We don't have him here in South Lick, but that don't mean Anne don't have him in the sheriff's clink over to Nashville."

By now Danna had joined us. I sniffed. And swore, turning back to the grill. While I was neglecting my job, the pancakes had burned on the bottom. I scraped them into the compost bucket and started over. A couple of other orders were done, so I plated them up.

"What did you say?" Danna asked Buck.

"I said we don't have Rowling in the South Lick jail, but the sheriff might could be detaining him."

"All night long?" she screeched.

"Now, now, Miss Danna," Buck said, making a slow-down gesture with his hand. "Don't get your britches in a twist. I'll do you a favor and make a call to Detective Henderson, once I get some sustenance into me."

"You will?" she asked.

He nodded.

"Thank you," Danna said. "You're the best."

"Miss?" a customer called from across the room.

"These are ready, Danna." I pointed to the full plates. "We both need to get back to work."

She nodded as she grabbed the plates. Buck strolled to his favorite table, hands in his pockets. I probably should just put a RESERVED sign on it, he was in here that often. I assembled his usual order, gargantuan in proportion. Two over easy, a stack of pancakes, four pieces of bacon, wheat toast, two biscuits with sausage gravy, and a muffin. I knew he'd eat every bite and still have room for lunch later. Danna was busy, so I carried it over to him, and he thanked me.

"Danna's really worried about Isaac," I said in a low voice, my back to the other diners nearby. "She thinks he might have been murdered, too."

"Welp, you know what *think* did. Followed a dust-cart and thought it was a wedding." He took a huge bite of muffin. "Mmm. This muffin is granny-slappin' good. Tell you what. I'll go ahead and call right now, put that girl's mind at ease." He wiped his hands and pulled out a phone.

"Thanks. I have to get back to the grill. Let Danna know what you hear, okay?"

He nodded and I went back to my cooking. I saw Danna hovering near Buck. I saw Buck speak to her. I saw her posture collapse in dejection. The news could be that her man was locked up. Or it could be Henderson didn't have him. I was pretty sure she hadn't been told he'd been murdered, though. She would be in a lot worse shape if she had.

Chapter Thirty

It wasn't until after eight that I had a chance to ask Danna what Buck had said. Turner had arrived on time and taken over at the grill after I'd filled him in on Danna's worries. Buck had consumed every crumb of his hungry-man's breakfast and left a few minutes ago.

"Nobody knows where Isaac is," she said, her arms full of dishes. "Buck called the detective, but she doesn't have him. Buck says his people will keep an eye out for him around the area. But if Isaac doesn't want to be found or is in trouble somewhere, they're not going to spot him going shopping or filling up his truck with gas or anything."

"And Isaac's mom?" I asked. "Were you able to reach her?"

Danna shook her head. "I dug up a number for her on the Web, but when I called it was disconnected. She must have canceled her landline."

"You don't know where she works?"

"Ize didn't really talk about his family much, except recently telling me his dad got out of prison.

I called his father at the halfway house. Isaac isn't there, either. Robbie, I don't know what to do."

"I'm sorry, Danna. I'm sure he'll turn up."

Turner, who had been following our conversation, said, "Is there an old hunting shed on his property? Maybe he's hiding out there." He gave a wry smile.

Earlier in the spring his own father had done exactly that.

Danna narrowed her eyes. "He does own ten acres. I have no idea if there's a shed out there in the woods."

"Remind me where his house is," I said.

"It's off the road to Helmsburg. You know, Route 45. I wish I could . . ." She glanced around the full, buzzing restaurant. "Nah, never mind."

"You wish you could go hunt for him. I know the feeling. If we get a good midmorning lull, you can take off for an hour or two, but I really need you now. Does that work?"

"Thanks." Her strained face relaxed a notch. "I'll make it up to you."

Turner dinged the bell indicating an order was ready, even though Danna and I were standing only feet away. A customer caught my gaze and pointed to her coffee cup. Four women pushed through the door from outside. A couple at a table full of empty dishes stood, ready for their check. We really didn't have time to stand around chatting about a missing boyfriend. And I wasn't so sure it was safe for Danna to go traipsing through unfamiliar woods in search of a man, possibly PTSD-beset, whom the detective considered a person of interest in Pia's murder.

Roberto and Maria came downstairs a few minutes

later. All the tables were full, so I took them each a cup of coffee, dosed with sugar and cream as I'd learned they both preferred it. Maria thanked me and took her mug into the cookware area.

"There will be a memorial service for Pia this afternoon at IU," I told Roberto. "Do you and Maria want to go?"

"I will ask her. I think she will say yes. You are going, too?"

I nodded. "If you want to go, I'll go with you. I can show you on a map a couple side trips you could do today before the service, if you want. Down to French Lick and the restored casino. Or out east to Columbus, which has lots of cool architecture."

"I will ask my wife. But after breakfast I have coffee with Don."

"Right. How is Maria doing?" I asked my father. "You know, that thing she read in the Italian news last night?"

"She is concerned, but we can do nothing until we return."

"You still have no idea how they learned you were here?"

"No, but I have the suspicion. The man Maria's brother did wrong to? He has been following my wife." He kept his voice low and gazed after Maria.

"Like following her around?"

"No, but how do you say . . . keeping the track on her."

"Keeping track of her."

"Yes. Where she goes, what she does. I think this man knows we are here. He looks up the news on the Internet. He tells a false story to the newspaper."

"Can't you get a restraining order on him? You know, complain to the police this guy is harassing Maria."

He shook his head. His deep brown eyes, so exactly like mine, pulled down with worry. "She won't let me go to *polizia*. It is a difficult situation, Robbie. And the man, he is cousin to Pia."

My eyes flipped wide open. "Pia's cousin?" How intertwined could this murder get? I wondered if the detective knew about that connection. If she did, she might also suspect Maria and Roberto of killing Pia to get back at the stalker cousin. Which made no sense at all, of course.

Danna caught my gaze and beckoned.

"I'm really sorry to hear that, *Babbo*. I have to get back to work now, but the next table that opens up is yours." I gave him a quick hug and hurried back to my business. I topped off coffees and carried plates full of omelets and biscuits and bacon to hungry diners. I freed Danna to whip up more blueberry muffins since they'd proved so popular we already were running low. But my mind stayed on Maria's stalker. How terrible to have somebody with a grudge who tracked your every movement, which was made easy by the Internet. And to distrust the authorities so much you didn't want to ask them for help.

Chapter Thirty-one

Roberto and Maria had lingered over breakfast, him reading the *Brown County Democrat*, her perusing her phone. Twenty minutes ago a touring van had driven up, and fifteen women poured into my establishment, exclaiming over the charming store, the vintage cookware, and how delicious the menu items sounded. Maybe they'd seen my ad in the bluegrass festival program book. Directly after they arrived, the delivery person had buzzed at the service door, so Asian noodles or the Hot Brown could be our lunch special if we ever got time to prepare them.

I glanced at Danna and shook my head, mouthing, "Sorry." No way I could let her go on an Isaac hunt this morning. My other B&B guests would probably be down shortly, too. At least Chase would.

Her shoulders slumped and despair tinted her eyes, but she didn't argue with me.

Don walked in the door at ten o'clock sharp. I greeted him and pointed to where Roberto still sat. Maria had gone back upstairs a few minutes earlier.

"I'll bring coffee, Don. Are you going to eat, too?"

"I think I just might. I'm pretty partial to blue-berries." He smiled and headed to my father's table with more of a spring in his step than I'd ever seen. Looked like confession was good for the soul. Or maybe it was his conscience it benefited.

Getting the ladies group seated and fed took the three of us much of the next hour. From Kentucky, they were as delightful as they said my store was. One told me she'd heard of us and had organized members of the Louisville Culinary Club to come up here on a field trip. Too bad the Bluegrass Omelet had been yesterday's special, not today's.

Chase trotted down the interior steps and slid into a seat at the last available table. I worried the next time the door bell jangled. If it was another van of tourists, they were going to have to wait. Instead, the customer was Anne Henderson. She waved to me and strode straight to Chase's table. How did she know he'd just come downstairs? Maybe she'd made an appointment to talk with him further.

I carried over the coffeepot for Chase—and for my own curiosity. "Good morning, Chase and Detective Henderson. Coffee for both of you?" Henderson hadn't sat yet.

"I'll take some, thanks." Chase blinked at Henderson. "Can I help you, Detective?"

So it wasn't an appointment, after all.

"I had a few more questions for you and you haven't been responding to my messages. May I sit?"

He waved at the other chair. "Be my guest," he said, but he didn't sound too happy about it. He pulled a phone out of his shirt pocket and widened his eyes.

"Well, would you just look at that? I turned it off last night and forgot to switch it back on this morning."

Henderson nodded once, slowly, kind of like she didn't believe him, and took the chair opposite. She glanced up at me. "I'd love some coffee, thank you."

I poured for each. "I'll be back to get your orders in a minute."

"Only coffee for me," the detective said.

"And I'll have what I had yesterday," Chase added.

"Granola, yogurt, and fruit. Got it." I stepped away. I didn't have an excuse in the world to stand there and eavesdrop, so I took the coffeepot around to other tables until it was empty. When I returned to the cooking area to start another pot, I caught Danna looking longingly at Henderson, like she couldn't wait to talk to her about Isaac.

"Danna, fix a healthy plate and take it to Chase, please." She could ask Henderson if there was any news while she was there.

I helped Turner plate up the last of the ladies' meals and carried them to a four-top.

One of them, a blue-haired matron, smiled at me. "We love what y'all have done with the store, Miz Jordan. We come up here a couple few years ago and this place was the saddest thing, all run down."

I nodded. It had been neglected, for sure. Running the store had gotten too much for Jo, the previous owner, and she'd been glad to unload it for a reasonable price into my hopeful hands. That she also handed over the treasure trove of antique kitchen implements was a double plus for me, and I had Adele to thank for inviting me to check out the place after Mom died. I loved that I was pretty much living my dream, at least when murder didn't interfere.

"I'm glad you came back, and I hope we'll see you again," I responded. "The leaves are really something to see in the fall."

"Oh, we know. We'll be back for sure, won't we, girls?"

Her friends all nodded.

"We heard about Miz Berry's death," Blue Hair went on. "She was my cousin's brother-in-law's sister. What a crying shame, and so soon after her own daughter's murder. They anywheres near finding the evil person who ended Miz Berry's life?"

My gaze shifted to the detective, and then back to my customer. "I'm not sure."

"But aren't you a private detective? You helped catch the scoundrel who killed Erica, my cousin said."

The rest of the ladies were rapt, gazing at me in awe. *Sheesh.*

I had to nip this in the bud immediately. "No, not at all. I'm a chef and a carpenter. It was the police who solved the case. Exactly like they will this one, too. Enjoy your meals, ladies." I smiled and turned away.

At Chase's table, Henderson sat erect, her tablet in front of her, but it didn't look like Chase was saying anything. Danna arrived with Chase's breakfast. I was too far away to hear what she asked the detective. Whatever the reply was apparently gave Danna a bit of hope. I met her back at the kitchen area.

"She said she could send someone out to check

out his property, because it's in unincorporated territory," Danna said a bit breathlessly. "At least that's something. I just want to know what happened to him."

"Good, then." I surveyed the restaurant. There were no urgent needs at the moment. "Danna, why don't you take five or ten minutes break. Turner, you go after her, okay? I'll take the grill if anybody new comes in."

"Aye-aye, skipper," Turner said.

Danna headed off for the ladies' room. I pushed a couple of unclaimed sausages onto the cooler end of the grill and started a pot of water to boil for the noodles. I could cool them down quickly in ice water when they were done. I forked up one of the sausages and ate it standing, I was so hungry. As I did, I spied Chase rise, shaking his head at Henderson. Whatever she wanted, he wasn't delivering. Because he didn't know, or because he didn't want to share?

He slid his hands in his pockets and strolled toward me. "I won't be back until late tonight," he said as he passed.

"Enjoy your day," I replied.

"Not sure it's the best business practice to let a sheriff's detective make this her second office, you know," he said in an officious tone.

Yeah. Don't tell me what to do, buddy. I merely smiled. "Catching a murderer or two takes a pretty high priority. If it will help her, I'm all for it."

He rolled his eyes but didn't contradict me, and headed for the front door.

I saw a hand waving. It was Henderson's hand, so I trucked over there.

"Ms. Jordan, I am also very interested in speaking with Beth Ferguson, who is also not responding to my messages. Could you possibly take me to her room?"

"Are you going to search it?"

"No, I don't have a warrant. But I do have some questions. Perhaps knocking will achieve what a voice mail has not."

Danna had emerged from the restroom.

"Sure, one second." I went over and asked Turner to hold off on his break for a couple of minutes, and asked Danna to cover for me. "I shouldn't be long. The detective wants to check something upstairs. Oh, and the pot of water is for the soba."

They both nodded

"And the Hot Brown sandwich for the special today?" Danna asked.

"Let's do it tomorrow, instead. I don't think we have time for both." I grabbed the master keys from my desk and led Henderson up the stairs and to Beth and Ed's room. I knocked. "Beth? Ed? Can you open the door, please?" I listened but got no response. "They might have already gone out for the day," I murmured to Henderson. I knocked again, louder and longer. "Beth?"

The door to my father's room opened instead, and Maria stuck her head out. "What it is?" She held a hairbrush and had applied a new coat of lipstick. Her eyes widened and her face paled when she saw the detective.

"We're trying to get them to open the door," I said.

She shook her head. "Not there. They go out, maybe thirty *minuti*. They drive."

"Thanks, Maria."

She shut the door before I was barely finished speaking, clicking the lock shut. I was pretty sure she didn't want to join the line of people Henderson was questioning. I held up my master key.

"Want to peek?" I asked Henderson.

The detective held up both hands. "As long as you're clear it wasn't at my instigation."

"Clear." I fit the key in the lock and pushed the door open. And then stared. They'd left the room as messy as before, but all their personal belongings were gone. No shoes, no suitcases. I checked the bathroom. No Dopp kit or cosmetics case.

I turned back to Henderson. "They weren't going to check out until Sunday. They're gone."

Again she nodded once, slowly. "Very interesting. I assume they didn't stiff you for the bill?"

"No. I have their credit card information. I've already turned away guests who wanted to come only for the weekend, so you can be sure I'll charge my early departures the whole amount." I ought to keep back a cleaning fee, too. "I have Ed's home address downstairs if you want it."

"That would be very helpful, Ms. Jordan. Very helpful indeed."

"Detective, while we're alone, I should tell you that Beth and Sue Berry had an argument Tuesday night at the festival."

"Oh?"

"Sue accused her of sneaking into the festival without paying. Beth said she'd forgotten her purse. I doubt that's motive to murder someone, but Ed told me Beth was prone to throwing fits, to sudden anger."

"Funny, he didn't tell me that," Henderson said.

"But he told you she went out on long solo runs in the mornings?"

"Yes, he admitted as much."

"I also wondered if Beth and Sue might have had some kind of run-in in the past. Yesterday when I asked Beth if she'd known Sue before, she nearly lost it with me. It seemed like she was lying when she said she hadn't."

"Ms. Jordan, please remember that I am a trained officer of the law, specifically a homicide detective. You are not to question persons of interest." Her dark eyebrows came together as she stared at me.

"Of course not. It was just a casual question." I drew one hand behind me and crossed my fingers at my own little lie. "Have you made any progress on either murder? I'd hate to think my father and step-mother were sleeping up here on the same floor as a killer." I kept my voice low, not that I thought Maria was listening in, or that she'd understand if she was.

Henderson let out the smallest of sighs. "I can't share such information with a civilian. Surely you know that by now." She regarded me with tilted head.

"Of course I know, but I'm concerned for my family."

"I will mention I am somewhat dismayed at Mr. Rowling's disappearance. These two characters, as well." She gestured at the Sapphire room. "I mentioned to Rowling he needed to stay in the county and be available."

"We're all concerned that he's missing, at least

Danna and I are. You know he's a veteran who was deployed to the Middle East, right?

"Very much aware, thank you. And I'm well versed in the reactions those suffering from PTSD can experience."

"Of course." She clearly wasn't going to tell me a thing, and I didn't seem to have anything new to tell her, either. "I'd better be getting back to my customers." At her nod, I locked the door again.

I realized I needed to find another B&B owner to ask what the protocol was when your guests check out two days early. Should I clean the room today and hope someone else still wanted it for the weekend, or leave it as is in case Beth and Ed—or one of them—came back before Sunday noon? They still had the keys, too. I sighed. I'd have to change the lock now. Maybe I should check into how big hotels programmed those key cards. Except I didn't have time to think about any of it until after I closed today.

Chapter Thirty-two

Nothing had blown up downstairs in my absence, thank goodness. After we descended from checking out Beth and Ed's room, I jotted down Ed's home address from the slip he'd filled out when he and Beth registered. I included his license plate number, which I also required from guests, and the make and model of his car.

I handed Henderson the piece of paper. "I didn't get Beth's address, unfortunately, and Ed said they don't live together."

"Please inform me if they happen to resurface," Detective Henderson said.

"I promise. Before you go, could you also take a look at my back door? I heard noises in the night and I think somebody tried to break in."

She gave me one of those stern *Seriously?* looks. "You didn't call it in."

"I didn't realize that was what I was hearing in the night. Obviously whoever did it wasn't successful. I just remembered it while I was getting ready to open this morning and we've been almost too busy to breathe since then."

"I'll check it out."

"Thank you." I listened to the bell jangle after her without any real hope of the police learning from the scratches on the lock plate. I pointed to Turner. "Break time."

Danna took over on the grill and I circulated among the tables asking if I could get the ladies something else. My blue-haired friend beckoned me over.

"I knew it," she said with an air of excitement. "You went upstairs with the lady sheriff to look for clues, didn't you?"

I shook my head. "Not really. She wanted to talk with two of my B&B guests, but they weren't there."

"Girls," she addressed her friends, none of whom could be any younger than sixty. "Next time, we'll have to stay here in Miz Jordan's B&B. Maybe we can be amateur sleuths, too!"

"Is there anything else I can get you today?" I asked, ignoring their eagerness to go all Nancy Drew on me. Or Miss Marple, more accurately.

"I think we'll just take the check, thanks," said Blue Hair, after checking with her tablemates. "This has been a pure delight, Miz Jordan."

"I'm glad you enjoyed it. I have a reservation system on my Web site for the rooms, so be sure you look at that if you're interested in staying here. I'd be happy to have you." *Maybe.* I laid their ticket on the table.

Don and Roberto stood and exchanged a hearty man-hug and a handshake before Don left.

"I go upstairs for a bit," Roberto told me. "Then

Maria and I will walk around town. We don't need the driving trip. This is fine with you?"

"You bet. I'm glad you and Don were able to re-connect."

"I also." My father beamed and headed for the stairs.

As I watched him go, I realized I hadn't talked with Henderson about Maria's stalker, and the fact that he was Pia's cousin. Maybe I'd subconsciously withheld that bit. I didn't want Maria to have any involvement in this case. The police might think differently, though. For now I was going to let them do their own research on Maria Fracasso.

The next half hour was spent taking money and making change for food and vintage cookware. Danna cleaned up while Turner chopped vegetables and threw together a massive bowl of spicy Asian noodles. The combo of snap peas, slivered red sweet pepper, and julienned carrot in tangy slightly sweet, slightly spicy dressing of rice vinegar, soy sauce, peanut oil, and a bit of sugar all mixed into buckwheat soba noodles was a hit. What Hoosiers called spicy wouldn't even be on the mild scale in southern California, but hey, when in Indiana, do as the Hoosiers do. If I added a few more drops of habanero sauce to my serving, that was my business.

It wasn't until eleven-thirty that the restaurant completely emptied out, although it was still full of the enticing aromas of bacon, blueberries, and biscuits.

"I hope the lunch rush is late today," I said, plopping into a chair with a thrown-together grilled cheese-and-bacon sandwich on a plate in front of me.

My helpers joined with their own meals, a classic two-over-easy with toast and sausage for Danna and a cheese omelet with the last blueberry muffin for Turner. The three of us munched in silence for a couple minutes.

"Turner," I began, "I think I'd like to take some food over to Glen Berry later. Think there's enough noodle salad for me to save some out for him?"

"Sure. If we run out, I'll whip up more. It doesn't take very long, and we have plenty of everything."

I thanked him and popped in my last bite as the door bell jangled. So much for our rest. I stood and turned to see Abe strolling toward our table. I sat again, smiling and patting the chair next to me.

"Hey, guys," he said, sliding into the chair. Greetings were exchanged all around, including a kiss on the cheek for me. "I got off early today, and where better to eat lunch than here?" He wore the green shirt of the rural electrical cooperative, a color that suited him.

Turner started to stand but Abe waved him down. "No rush. Looks like you all are taking your break. I'm not so hungry I can't wait a few minutes." He regarded Danna. "I was working out on Route 135 this morning near Story, and I saw your man."

The road to Story—the former town which now was a successful restaurant and inn—was also where Abe's parents lived.

Danna, who had been swiping up egg yolk with a piece of toast, whipped her head up. "You did? You saw Isaac?"

"Yup."

"Where was he?" she asked.

"I was down near where Stone Head used to be."

The hundred-and-eighty-year-old Stone Head had been a delightful sight. It was the oddest road marker I'd ever seen, a carved man's head with a Mona Lisa smile, crossed arms with hands pointing in opposite directions. Carved into the front and sides were the mileages to towns at all points of the compass. It had been vandalized more than once, but the last time, the head had never been found. Now a local man had carved a gravestone memorializing the marker.

"Rowling was in his truck ahead of me coming back this way," Abe went on. "You know how the road jogs left at the Stone Head site? He went straight instead, onto Bellsville Pike."

"Wow, man," Danna said. "Thank you, thank you, thank you." She got up and threw her arms around Abe for a moment, then stood back, eyes agleam.

"Did you lose him or something?" Abe looked puzzled and glanced at me.

"Yeah. Well. Never mind," Danna said. "I'm so relieved he's okay."

"Was he alone in the truck?" I asked. I popped in my last bite of pickle. If he'd been seeing a woman other than Danna, that could explain his not responding to her calls and texts last night.

"As far as I know he was."

Whew. "Danna, you should text Buck, and I'll let Detective Henderson know." I added for Abe's benefit, "Danna thought maybe something had happened to Isaac, and I think Henderson thought he was evading the authorities."

"Robbie, he didn't kill that woman. Either of them!" Danna stood and glared down at me.

"Danna, down girl. I said *Henderson* thought he might have, not that *I* thought so." Although I still wasn't totally convinced of Isaac's innocence, and it was going to be interesting to hear where he'd been when he surfaced. "Just text Buck, okay?"

She nodded and walked away a few feet to work on her phone. Turner, who had been taking all this in, calmly finished his meal and stacked up all the plates then deposited them in the sink. I'd be willing to bet he was relieved not to play any part in the current drama. The murder a few months ago had included enough family drama to last him years.

"Let me text Henderson," I told Abe.

"Do what you gotta do, Robbie. I'll still be here." He smiled, and his dimple made me want to drop everything and drag him into my apartment. I smiled back and took out my phone, instead.

Chapter Thirty-three

The Asian noodles were a success with the lunch crowd, which was surprisingly light. I had plenty of time to mull over Beth and Ed clearing out but not checking out. Maybe being questioned by the detective had pushed Beth over the edge and she'd demanded to be taken home. Maybe they'd found a place to stay nearer to the festival venue, but I doubted it. Lodging was usually sold out for miles around way in advance way of the festival. Fast approaching was the final weekend with big-name stars being showcased. I might never know where the couple had gone, or why.

After Abe finished his lunch, he left enough money to cover the check and then some, and gave me a quick kiss. "I'm going home for a couple hours. Get cleaned up, pay some bills, that kind of thing. What time do you want me back to take you to the memorial service?"

I'd asked him earlier if he would go with me and he'd said of course he would.

"Are you sure you want to go?" I now queried.

"Robbie." He laid his hands on my shoulders and looked me in the eye. "If you want me to go with you, then I want to. Okay?" He smiled encouragingly.

"Okay. It's just that you had a disagreement with her, and—"

"And that's all it was. I didn't have any problems with her as a person—heck, I barely knew her—and she was a good musician. What matters to me is right now. So what time should I be back?"

I loved this guy and could barely believe my luck at finding him. Or had he found me? "Actually, I wanted to take some food over to Glen beforehand. Can you be here by three? I'd appreciate the company." If there was one thing I'd learned from the past murders, it was not to do foolish things like visiting a potential killer alone.

"That's a nice gesture."

Nice? Maybe. But I also wanted to see if Glen would act like the grieving husband or like a murderer covering up his evil actions.

"Three o'clock it is. With bells on," he added.

I laughed. "You can probably leave the bells at home." We said our good-byes and a moment later the cowbell on the door jangled after him. I turned back to my business. It was Friday and a slow lunch. I hadn't been to the bank all week and the profits from the week were piling up in the safe in my apartment. I headed over to Danna and Turner.

"I'm going to run out to the bank. This doesn't look like anything the two of you can't handle, right?"

Danna gave me two thumbs up. "We got it, boss lady."

Turner nodded his agreement, so I aimed myself

for my apartment. I took a few minutes to freshen up, eat an apple, and play with Birdy, whom I felt I'd been neglecting this week. Well, my parents would be gone tomorrow or the next day, and then I'd have my day off. I gave the kitty a rain-check stroke on the head, then filled two zippered bank bags with the cash from the last few days and slid them into a shoulder bag.

"See ya tonight, Birdman," I told my kitty, who rested sphinxlike with his head up but his eyes closed. He opened one eye to a slit, and his ears moved, then he stilled again.

I went back through the restaurant and was almost to the front door when it opened in front of me. Isaac stood in the entrance, nearly filling the space with his bulk.

"Hi, Robbie," he said in his deep, soft voice. For such a big guy, he spoke with one of the gentlest voices I'd ever heard. "Can you spare Danna for a couple minutes?"

"Come in and shut the door, Isaac," I said. "We've been having a fly problem." That was a half-truth, but mostly I wanted to hear what he said to Danna.

As he obliged, I surveyed the restaurant. One new group of three had come in while I was in my apartment, but otherwise only four tables were occupied and they'd all been served. I could postpone my trip to the bank.

"Sure I can spare her." I took another look at him. His eyes looked haunted. Was it the dark shadows beneath them, or a dark look in them? "Are you all right?"

"I am." His gaze was fixed on Danna's back as she stood at the grill.

I stared when he brought his hand up to rub his forehead. The hand had fresh cuts on it, especially in the purlicue, the soft space where his thumb met the rest of his hand.

When he didn't say anything else, I offered, "I'll get her."

I hurried over to the kitchen area. "Danna, you have a visitor. Take a few minutes break. I'll wait to go to the bank."

She whirled. Her eyes went wide, and she wiped her hands on her apron as she strode to Isaac. They stood with arms around each other for a moment. I finally had to avert my eyes at such a private vignette. When I looked again, they'd moved almost out of sight behind the cookware shelves. I stashed my bag under the counter, washed my hands, and got to work.

I jotted down the new customers' orders while Turner did dishes. After I'd carried over the three-some's two burgers with coleslaw and one order of Asian noodles with a grilled cheese and tomato sandwich, I busied myself busing a few tables. Still Danna and Isaac hadn't emerged. I glanced at the wall clock. They'd been talking for fifteen minutes.

I'd taken a couple's money and thanked them when Danna hurried toward me. I stepped away from the table.

"Robbie, you have to talk to him. He won't listen to me." She was half breathless and rushed her whispered words. "I told him he has to tell the detective where he's been. He says it's none of her business."

"Did he tell you where he was?"

She shook her head hard. "I'm sure he didn't do anything wrong. I know it."

"I doubt I'll be able to convince him if you can't."

"Will you at least try?" She glanced over at the cookware area. "Before he disappears again?"

I nodded and walked toward him, trying to figure out how to approach this gentle but clearly conflicted man. I came around the end of one row of shelves to find Isaac gazing out the front window, fists clenched. *Uh-oh.*

I scuffled a foot on the ground, making a noise before I spoke so I didn't startle him. "Hey, Isaac." I kept my tone casual.

He turned slowly. "Robbie."

I cleared my throat. "Isaac, you know Detective Henderson is looking for you, right?"

He stiffened. "So? Does she have a warrant for my arrest?" His face got that flat look again.

"Not that I know of. She's simply trying to follow up all possible leads in the murders."

He leaned his head forward a little and light reentered his expression. "Murders plural? There was another one?"

Could he really not know? "Yes. Sue Berry was killed yesterday morning."

He took in a sharp breath. "Not Ms. Berry. She was such a nice lady." His eyes shifted left and right under a frowning brow, as if he was searching for something in his mind. His huge hands unclenched. He focused on me again. "Oh, I am so screwed," he murmured, almost to himself. "I am so very screwed."

Chapter Thirty-four

I stared at Isaac. "What do you mean?" Surely he wasn't saying he was screwed because he'd actually killed Sue. What possible motive would he have?

He let out the deepest, longest sigh I'd ever heard. He met my gaze with those unusual eyes of his. "I mean because I was having one of my . . . uh, incidents."

"What's an incident?"

"It's when my PTSD flares up. I have to go off by myself and I barely remember where I've been or what I've done. The cops are going to have an effing field day with that."

I wrinkled my nose. I imagined they would.

"When I feel one coming on, I've learned to go into the woods and stay there until I feel normal again. Early on I didn't know how to deal, and I got into some pretty bad bar fights. So the woods is where I was."

That must be where he'd gotten the cuts on his hand. I hoped. "So your being in the woods coping is

the reason you stood Danna up and weren't answering
your phone or texts? Does she know this about you?"

He winced. "That's the reason. I wanted to tell her
but hadn't gotten around to it yet. She's a great girl,
and I'm damaged goods." He seemed to have shrunk
a few inches all the way around. "And now . . . it's all
too big to explain."

"She is great, I agree. And too smart not to sympa-
thize." I patted his arm. "Tell her. She really likes you.
She'll understand."

"I guess."

"Then call the detective. It only looks worse the
longer you don't get back to her. Promise?"

He nodded somberly. "All right." He took another
look at me. "How'd you get so people smart, Robbie?
You're a cook. A carpenter. You're younger than me,
I think, or nearly the same age. But you sound like
some wise teacher. A guru."

I did? "I don't feel like one. But thanks, I guess.
Let me go get Danna."

When he nodded, I scurried away. "Go," I told
Danna. "He has something to tell you."

I watched her head back to her man. Isaac might
need a lawyer, too, but at least he was being honest
now. That counted for a lot.

Before I could turn back to the myriad tasks running a restaurant entails, the front door opened
again, to admit Adele. I lifted a hand in greeting and
started toward her, kissing her soft papery cheek
when I got there.

"Are you here for lunch?" I asked.

She glanced around with a furtive air. She grabbed

my arm, pulling me close. "I have something to tell you," she whispered.

"And it's a state secret?" I murmured.

"No lip, now," she scolded. "Seriously, you got a minute?"

"That's about all I have."

"I paid a visit to Gail."

"Who's Gail?"

"Gail Broward. Chase Broward's wife. Remember I told you we were in a wood-carving club together?" She kept her voice low, but at least she'd stopped whispering.

I nodded.

"So I thought I'd stop by, say hey, see what she knew of her husband's shenanigans. We got to talking, one thing led to another, and don't you know, she told me she took and put a tracking device on his car without him knowing."

My eyes went wide and my jaw dropped. "She did?" This could be really important. Maybe the break in the case Detective Henderson needed.

"Yup. She can check on him from her computer any time she wants."

"She needs to tell the detective. Has she?"

"Precisely what I said to her. Gail told me she doesn't want to get him in trouble with anybody else except her."

"But the tracker could show if he went out again that night, either night," I said. "Where he went. When he came back here." She had to tell Henderson, and soon.

"Exactly." Adele nodded, her eyes twinkling.

"Did she tell you what she saw on the tracker?"

"No. She said her lips were sealed on the matter. But how come you don't know Broward's comings and goings? You're a landlady now. Or an innkeeper, more so."

"I know. But I don't hear a thing from my apartment. And the parking and outside door for the guests are on the far side of the building. I'm going to put a camera up on that side but I haven't had time to yet."

"Anyhoo, I steered my conversation with Gail around to passwords," Adele went on.

What? "Why in the world would you talk about passwords?"

"She told me hers was GailChase1997. The year they met."

"And you talked about passwords why?" I asked again, wishing I could hurry her up.

A new party of four had come in. Two tables were finished and gathering their things. The smell of overdone hamburger wafted my way. Turner was moving as fast as he could, but with neither Danna nor me helping him, he was starting to throw frantic looks at me.

"So Phil can tap into her computer. Find out where Broward went. Then we'll crack the case." Adele looked inordinately pleased with herself.

"You want Phil to hack in remotely." Was it even possible? "Adele, that's crazy. All we have to do is tell the detective. She'll subpoena the system or whatever they need to do."

"But then Gail won't never speak to me again." My aunt set fists on hips and pressed her lips together.

I shook my head. She and I rarely came into conflict and I didn't quite know how to handle it. So I took the chicken's way out. "I have to get back to work. Thanks for telling me. Can you hold off on asking Phil to hack in, please?"

"Too late." Her tone was borderline triumphant. "I already did."

Chapter Thirty-five

By two o'clock the restaurant was empty. "I'm running out to the bank," I told Danna and Turner. "I'll help with the cleanup when I get back, and then you both can leave early, okay? It's Friday, after all."

"You're the boss," Danna said, grinning at Turner.

"Boss," he finished, then gave Danna a high five.

"Geez, you guys," I said with a laugh. "Give me a break." Cleaning up wouldn't take long, since they were good with wiping down and scrubbing as they cleared tables and cooked. On my way out I turned the sign to CLOSED half an hour before the posted closing time.

Danna's mood had lightened considerably after her second conversation with Isaac. He'd left, and Danna told me he planned to head over to the sheriff's office and tell the detective where he'd been. *Good*. One murky question answered. I hoped.

My own mood had darkened after Adele's visit. Phil should not be hacking into anybody's computer. He could get into big trouble for hacking, especially if the goal was to find information Adele could pass

along to the police. I'd sent him a text saying exactly
that but I hadn't heard back. Adele had left after
saying she'd see me at Pia's memorial service. I'd
asked her if she'd known Pia and she said no, but
maybe the murderer would be there.

"And you would know this how?" I'd asked.

"Clues, my dear. Clues." With that she'd bustled
out the door, acting way too cheerful.

Clues. *Right.* My aunt was getting out of hand.
Was this how the homicide detective viewed my own
efforts?

Once I'd returned and Turner and Danna were
on their way to whatever their Friday held next, I
gathered the restaurant laundry and headed into my
apartment for a little downtime. I started a load,
washed up, and changed into a memorial service
outfit. I'd checked the weather on the front porch
and the sunny day had turned breezy with clouds
scudding past, so I opted for black slacks, a simple
fuchsia silk shell, and a black and white linen jacket.
Somber but not grim. I brushed out my curly hair,
which I always had to tie back in the restaurant, and
left it loose on my shoulders. A bit of lip gloss, some
silver earrings, black sandals, and I was ready. Abe
was picking me up at a few minutes before three to
make our condolence visit to Glen. I would have
rather had a long, strenuous bike ride on such a
pretty day, but once again a ride wasn't in the cards
for this afternoon.

Shoot. I needed to give the detective a heads-up
on Gail's tracking device. I'd saved her number to
my phone, so I whipped it out and called her.

"Henderson." The name came out fast and curt.

"Detective, I learned something this afternoon I think you should know."

"Is it about Mr. Rowling? Because he's here."

"I'm glad he is. He promised me he would go right over." *Whew.* One thing had gone right, at least.

"He did, although the fact that no one saw him or can vouch for his whereabouts is frankly disturbing," she said. "So if not about him, why did you call?"

"My aunt, Adele Jordan, knows Gail Broward, Chase Broward's wife. Adele went to see her this morning. It turns out Gail suspected her husband was having an affair, so she secretly put some kind of GPS tracker on his car. I thought you should know."

"Very interesting. Was your aunt planning to let me know?"

I swallowed. "Um, well, I'm sure she was. The thing is, the wife didn't want to get her husband in trouble with anybody but her, so she didn't want Adele to tell you. I think Adele was worried about her friendship."

A snort came over the phone. "I'm sorry, but a double murder investigation trumps friendship every time. And you can tell your aunt I said so. I appreciate you coming forward."

Adele was going to kill me, but I knew it would only be figuratively. "Do you need Chase's home address?" I asked. "I have it on his paperwork."

"No, thank you. I have it, as well. Good-bye, Ms. Jordan."

"Wait." I caught her before she disconnected. "Do you know there's a memorial service for Pia this afternoon at Indiana University?"

Henderson sighed. "Yes, I'm aware of the service. Was there anything else?"

I said there wasn't. Of course she would know of the service. It was her job to keep track of things like that. After the call went dead, I texted Phil again.

Police know about tracker. Please don't hack.

There. I'd done my due diligence. I hadn't withheld potential evidence. I'd helped the police without getting into trouble myself. I hoped Phil would pay attention to my messages. I hoped he hadn't already started hacking. Most of all, I hoped the tracker would either clear or convict Chase Broward.

I made sure Birdy's food and water were in good shape and played with him as I munched a quick cheese sandwich. He ignored the few cat toys I'd purchased, preferring to chase a tinfoil ball. My gaze fell on my puzzle, which I'd left on the kitchen table yesterday. Had I learned anything new I could add? Actually, yes. The tracker Gail had attached to Chase's car. And Isaac's PTSD. I used the *T* in GUILTY to write PTSD going down. I added GAIL at the bottom of ALIBI and hung GPS off the G of GAIL.

But adding items to my crossword wasn't doing anything to actually solve the real puzzle. I might as well give up.

Chapter Thirty-six

Abe and I stood at Glen's front door at a couple of minutes past three listening to the doorbell chime within. I held a container of Asian noodles and a small sack filled with brownies. After their daughter had been murdered last fall, I'd also brought Glen and Sue comfort food. That time it had been a meatloaf and a pan of scalloped potatoes. Soba noodles wasn't exactly a traditional dish to bring a bereaved person around here, but I hadn't had time to whip up a casserole, or a covered dish, as most called it. And this time, sadly, the food was for Glen only.

I glanced at Abe. "I called earlier and he said he'd be here. Maybe he's not?"

"He could have had an emergency at one of his stores, I suppose." Abe pressed the bell again.

I thought I heard footsteps. A moment later the lock snicked and Glen pulled the door open. His lips were pressed flat and he frowned as if irritated. Once he saw who we were his eyebrows raised.

"We wanted to convey our sympathies, Glen."

"I'm really sorry for your loss," Abe added.

I proffered the container and the bag. "I brought you some food."

He shook his head slightly. "Thank you, Robbie. Afternoon, O'Neill." Glen's shirttails hung out and his feet were bare. His normally neat hair stuck up like he'd been sleeping. He extended his hands to receive the food.

"Are you doing all right?" I asked.

"Do I look like I'm doing all right?" he snapped.

Abe slid his hand into mine and squeezed. "It can't be easy, losing your wife."

Glen exhaled through his nostrils. "It's hell, that's what it is. The lady detective won't leave me alone, either. Keeps asking me questions about yesterday morning."

"What kinds of questions?" I tilted my head.

"Did I see Susie leave the house? Had we been arguing lately? Where are the keys to her car, and on and on. I keep telling her, how could I have seen my wife leave the house when I was out back playing my guitar? It's the one thing that keeps me sane when things are going badly elsewhere."

"I know what you mean, man," Abe said. "I feel the same about my banjo."

Huh. When things were going badly elsewhere. Was Glen's business failing? Or was he referring to his marriage?

"And of course her car keys are on the hook inside the door where we always keep them," Glen added.

"I wonder why she asked if you'd been arguing," I chimed in. "I've always thought you two were the model of a couple in harmony."

Glen's gaze shifted to a point over my shoulder.

"Of course we hadn't been fighting. No more than the usual couple's spats, anyway."

I glanced over at the driveway. Sue's little two-toned Mini Cooper sat in front of the garage with the sun glinting off the windshield. I pictured a map showing where we were and where her body was found. Glen's house was in a newish development of ranch houses and split-levels on the other side of town from my store. And Scarce O' Fat Ridge Road was out the other direction from my store, way too far from here for an early morning walk. Someone had to have given Sue a ride, and she had to have known the person if she was killed there. But if she was dead before she arrived at her final destination, she could have conceivably been killed in her bed.

I shook myself out of my musings. Abe and Glen had moved on to propounding on baseball prospects this season.

"Come on, dude," Abe said, smiling. "You know the Cards don't have a chance now they traded away their star catcher."

Glen scoffed. "And the Reds have better prospects? No way."

Since Indiana didn't have a major-league base-ball team, Hoosiers' allegiances were often split among teams from St. Louis, Cincinnati, and Chicago. And fans could argue their relative merits until the cows came home. Except we didn't have that kind of time right now. Glen clearly wasn't going to ask us in, and we had to get back, anyway. I needed to meet Roberto and Maria at the store so we wouldn't be late for Pia's service.

At the next pause in the conversation, I spoke up.

"Sorry to interrupt, but we need to get going. Did you know there's a memorial service for Pia Bianchi this afternoon?"

Glen blinked, pursing his lips. "Oh?"

"Yes, at the chapel on the IU campus. The music department is holding it."

"I see."

"Do you have something planned for Sue?" Abe asked.

"Paula says we need to. It all seems like too much right now, though." Glen shook his head. "I guess we'll have to start putting things in motion."

His daughter Paula had now lost three members of her family, leaving her with only her father and her baby daughter. "How is Paula doing?"

"She's a basket case, frankly. I think the only thing holding her together is the baby."

"Well, give her my best." I did a mental head slap. I hadn't even thought to bring Paula food, too. Maybe I could squeeze it in later. "Do let us know when the service will be, okay?"

"And if we can help," Abe said.

"I'll do that. Thanks for the food."

Abe extended his hand and shook Glen's. "You take care, now."

Glen stepped back and closed the door. The lock clicked shut. As we turned to go, I noticed what I hadn't when we'd arrived. The front yard, which last year had been trimmed and edged within an inch of its life, now looked unkempt and overgrown. The lawn sprouted broadleaf weeds and was not mown. A shrub had lost its perfect mounded shape. A broken limb dangled off the poplar tree near the sidewalk, hanging from one ribbon of bark. The clematis winding around the lamppost looked dry and forlorn.

Glen or Sue—or both—had been neglecting upkeep on the property. I wished I knew who was the gardener in the family. Who was the neat freak. And why things had changed.

Chapter Thirty-seven

The rustling and murmuring gradually quieted in the chapel on the IU grounds. Roberto, Maria, and I had squeezed into one of the pews at the very back after we'd rushed to arrive by four o'clock. We'd had to park off campus and hurry in through the Sample Gates, ignoring the impressive array of the original limestone buildings on the quad, now over 130 years old. The chapel itself was also built of limestone, with a steeply angled slate roof and a copper spire at one end. Abe had asked if I minded if he stayed home, saying he would prepare a nice dinner for the four of us. I'd said dinner sounded perfect, and I'd be with Roberto and Maria, anyway.

The decor inside was in a gleaming light-colored wood except for plain white walls, which were unadorned, leaving room for people of all faiths to worship. I spied Phil sitting near the aisle next to Adele and Samuel in the second row. The organ, which had been softly playing a piece I thought might be Vivaldi, also stilled. The light from outside illuminated the blues and reds of a star in a round stained-glass window near the peak of the ceiling. Two candelabras on a table at the front each held a dozen lit white candles.

A woman rose from the front pew, turning to face the mourners. She introduced herself as the chair of the music department. "We gather here today to celebrate the life of our friend, Pia Bianchi. Her musical path held great promise and was tragically cut short."

My father murmured a translation to Maria.

"I know her family in Italy would have liked to be here but they couldn't make it. To begin our service, Philostrate MacDonald will sing a tribute to his good friend. After that we welcome your remembrances. Please stand and use a loud and clear voice so all might hear." She sat.

Phil went forward and cleared his throat. "Pia loved this song, which Emmylou Harris wrote after her friend Kate McGarrigle died," he said in his deep resonant voice. "I changed the lyrics of 'Darlin' Kate' only a little. I sing it now for Pia."

Even from where I sat I could see his brilliant blue shirt bringing out the blue in his eyes.

He'd opened his mouth to start when the door at the rear opened and Anne Henderson slid in, closing it softly behind her. Not in uniform today, she wore a simple black jacket with a white blouse and gray pants. When she saw me looking at her, she gave a nod of recognition. She folded her hands in front of her and stood against the back wall, eyes roving over the assemblage.

Phil's strong lilting voice soared to the rafters, sure of note and surging with feeling. He came to what sounded like the chorus, singing about slipping the surly bonds of earth and sailing away, and that they might meet again somehow, someday. More than one person sniffed. Handkerchiefs and tissues became evident after a verse that said the singer wasn't sure where his friend had gone, but she would probably find a better song there.

My eyes were wet, too. From the beauty of Phil's voice in a beautiful building? From the tragedy of any life being cut short? From missing my mom, who didn't die at a murderer's hand but who also went too soon and too suddenly? If I had to bet, I'd say all of those. I gazed out the leaded glass window nearest me as the sun dimmed from a passing cloud.

Phil finished. He bowed his head and waited a moment before taking his seat. One by one, others stood and shared memories of Pia. A woman who said Pia had taught her to make ravioli, and that the recipe included an instruction to drink red wine while cooking. That got a laugh. A man, identifying himself as her voice teacher, mentioned that Pia worked harder than most students. After a half dozen more, a man sitting on the other side of the chapel stood.

I did a double take. A gray-suited Glen Berry? What was he doing here? He didn't even like Pia. Was this for show, to make a public appearance? He must have cleaned up and driven over here in a hurry. I shot a glance at the detective, who looked unfazed but had her full attention on Glen.

"My wife Sue befriended Pia. I'm here on Sue's behalf, since she also passed away this week." His voice broke and he stared at the floor for a moment, then took a deep breath and went on. "I know Susie would want me to say how much she would miss Pia, despite some rocky times they were having lately." He sat again with a heavy thud.

Interesting. Rocky times, absolutely. Tuesday night Sue had been furious with Pia. Would she really have missed the Italian? And was Glen truly as heart-broken over his wife's death as he was acting? I surveyed the backs of heads in the room. Was Chase here, too? Showing up would take a lot of nerve, especially since his liaison with Pia had been illicit. I didn't see him.

Our pew creaked as Maria stood, a white hand-kerchief twisted in her hands. "I visit from Italy." Her voice rang out.

In front of us, heads twisted to see who was speaking.

"I know Pia family. She was good girl. I pray for her soul." She crossed herself and sat, then slipped down to kneel, eyes shut, head bowed, her folded hands on the back of the pew in front.

A few people nodded, and a woman two rows up also crossed herself. I supposed I could share I'd been in a puzzle group with Pia, but I hardly knew her at all. I wasn't shy about speaking in public. You can hardly own a restaurant and not want to talk with people, all kinds of people. But I didn't have anything in particular to contribute, so I kept my mouth shut.

A guy who looked vaguely familiar stood, wiping a tear from his eye. His hair was pulled into a knot on top of his head like my recently departed guest. But this wasn't Ed. Where did I recognize him from?

"I've been playing music with Pia for a couple years," he began softly. When a white-haired lady cupped her hand to her ear, his voice grew stronger. "We didn't play your opera, or your, like classical stuff, what most of you folks probably prefer. Nah, we jammed with banjo, fiddle, spoons, washboard, you name it."

That's who he was. The fiddler in Abe's group at the festival the night before Pia was killed.

"That girl had talent," the speaker said. "Imma miss her so fuh . . . , I mean, Imma miss her like crazy, man."

A dead silence took over the airspace, followed by gasps and muttering.

The speaker wrinkled his nose and hung his head, like he'd realized what he'd almost said. "I mean it, you know? Pia could play. She could sing. She could compose. She was like, I don't know, the next 'Leonarda' da Vinci or something. Okay, that's all. Thanks for listening." He sank down in the pew, burying his face in his hands.

Abe and Pia had played the same kind of music, and both had played with this grieving man. Maybe my guy should have come instead of staying home to cook. At the least he could have comforted his fellow musician.

The department chair looked around, checking to see if anyone else had something to share. From a corner I hadn't been able to see, Chase Broward rose awkwardly, as if reluctant to do so.

I heard another gasp from two rows up, and a woman stood and stalked out. I was surprised he was here at all and amazed he apparently was going to speak publicly, but I shouldn't have been. The man was running for office, after all.

"Pia Bianchi was a fine person," he began in measured tones, hands clasped at his waist. "Immigrant. Musician. Friend to many. Her loss is a loss to the Indiana University community and to the bluegrass community. I had the honor of playing onstage with her and our friend who just spoke."

He nodded at Man-Bun, who turned and glared at Chase instead of acknowledging what they had in common. Clearly not actually a friend. Chase ignored the daggerly look. "We played with several others, too, the night before Pia was so horrifically taken from us."

He was really laying it on thick. Should I have expected anything else from a local politician with national aspirations? CUT TO THE CHASE WITH BROWARD, indeed.

"May she rest in God's love and find eternal peace," Chase finished.

I glanced back to see Henderson regarding Chase with a careful gaze.

The chairwoman stood. "That seems a suitable ending for our ceremony."

I heard an irreverent snort from someone but couldn't tell who had delivered it.

The chair continued. "I want to thank you all for coming to honor our friend. There will be light refreshments of the wine and cheese variety downstairs immediately following. Glen Berry has graciously donated the wine, and we thank him."

Glen dipped his head and raised his hand slightly in acknowledgment of the thanks.

The chair went on. "At six o'clock we're going to adjourn to DeAngelo's for a meal of the food Pia grew up eating, and you are all welcome to join us there. The restaurant owners, good friends of Pia's, have reserved the entire place for us."

Glen donated wine for the reception of a woman he despised. Well, bless his heart, as Adele would say.

Chapter Thirty-eight

It looked like nearly everyone from the service had filed downstairs for the wine and cheese. The room hummed with conversation and the air smelled of freshly baked cookies.

I balanced three glasses of white wine over to Roberto and Maria where they perched on chairs along the side of the room.

"I'll be back with a few appetizers," I said.

"*Grazie, Roberta,*" my father said.

Maria smiled her thanks. Her gaze slid to Anne Henderson, who stood talking with the department chair. Maria shuddered before looking away. She really did have a thing about the police.

I made my way to the end of the food table and found myself behind Phil. "What a lovely song you chose, Phil."

He twisted to see me. "Thanks, my friend. Pia deserved it."

"Funny how so many seemed to have loved her. But she rubbed nearly an equal number the wrong way," I murmured.

"She wasn't easy, I'll admit. But she had a good heart in there. I will truly miss her."

I hugged him with one arm, then we made our way down the table. I knew I was going straight to dinner after this. I stuck to carrots and celery and ignored my stomach. It wanted desperately to steer me toward the cheese and crackers I piled on a small plate for Roberto and Maria. I also avoided the already half-empty platter of cookies, despite their inviting aroma.

As I walked back across the room, I casually surveyed it. Glen Berry seemed to have left. I was surprised he'd even come to the service itself, and I didn't blame him for skipping this part of the ritual. He was going to have to endure another nearly identical gathering one day soon, except Sue's services would take place in Our Lady of the Springs, the Catholic church in town. The date would depend on when the police released Sue's body, I supposed. Which reminded me I still hadn't taken any food to Paula. Later tonight? Unlikely. I wanted to relax at dinner, and then I had food prep to do for tomorrow. Sunday night couldn't come too soon, the evening when prep wasn't part of my day because I closed the restaurant on Mondays. I loved my life, but it was also nice to take a break once in a while.

I delivered the food to Roberto and Maria, who were chatting in low voices in Italian, and picked up my wine. Clumps of Pia's friends and colleagues conversed in various formations. Phil and Man-Bun stood in a corner talking. Chase looked every inch the politician, wandering around introducing himself and shaking hands. Definitely a man running for office.

Adele and Samuel strolled toward us, each holding a glass of wine.

"Nice service, don't you think?" Adele asked Roberto. "Do they do this kind of thing where you come from, a purely memorial service?" She spoke clearly and not too fast to help the Italians understand. She didn't talk too loud and separate each word like Wanda had.

It must have worked, because Maria nodded. "Yes. Usually mass in church, but sometimes like this one, with friends and family."

Roberto drew out his phone and checked something. He glanced up. "Our flight, it goes tomorrow."

The ash issue must have cleared out quickly.

"We'll be sorry to have you go," Samuel said.

"Very," I added.

I left the four talking and moseyed over to where Anne Henderson stood alone against the wall, dying to ask her if she'd learned anything from Chase's wife's tracker. She probably wouldn't tell me, but it was worth a try.

"Ms. Jordan," she acknowledged. She held a bottle of water in lieu of a glass of wine

"Pretty good turnout, isn't it?" I gestured to the room.

"Mmm," she said, but her gaze was directed only at Chase.

"So were you able to get any useful information out of his wife's tracker?" I kept my voice down.

She gave me one of those *Oh, please* looks. "I'm not at liberty to say. As I expect you know by now. Or should know, anyway."

I smiled. "I was the one who told you about the tracker. I simply thought . . ." I flipped my hands open.

"We always welcome tips from helpful citizens, Ms. Jordan." She returned her gaze to Chase, who now approached Phil and the fiddler.

I looked at the men, too, halfway across the room, which wasn't particularly spacious. Chase shook Phil's hand and then offered a handshake to Man-Bun. The latter folded his arms instead and stared at Chase.

"I'm not shaking hands with you, Broward," he said, his voice loud and clear.

The conversation hushed around them. Chase took a step back, but the fiddler stuck to him.

"You think you're so slick, sliding along like an oily snake," he went on. "You, a married man, who spent a couple months doing it to a friend of mine and then dropped her without notice. You hurt Pia bad, man, and I'm never going to forget it. I'm going to make sure your wife doesn't forget it, either." His voice shook, grief mixing with rage.

Phil took his friend's elbow and turned him away. Chase stood with his hands in fists at his side. His smooth politician's mask had slid away, leaving a flared-nostril glower pointed at Man-Bun's back. As I watched, the mask slid back on. He straightened his tie, shot his cuffs, put on the whisper of a smile. He turned toward the door several yards away where the department chair stood, thanking people on their way out for coming.

The detective made it to Chase's side in a few brisk steps. "Mr. Broward, I need you to come with me."

She kept her voice down, but I was close enough to hear. The chairperson, even closer, widened her eyes.

"I'm afraid that won't be possible." Chase smiled and blinked. "I have a prior engagement."

"And I'm afraid you have no say in the matter. You can come quietly, or we can do this right here in public."

"Do what, Detective?" He gave a short laugh. "Arrest me?"

"Exactly." She pulled a pair of handcuffs out of her jacket pocket. "Chase Broward, you are under arrest for the murder of Pia Bianchi."

Chapter Thirty-nine

Abe lived in one of the Craftsman-style bungalows common in the area, which were built over a hundred years ago. A wide arched pass-through led from the living room to the dining room where we sat, Abe next to me, Roberto and Maria across from us. The windows were open to the mild air of the evening, with the distant drone of a lawnmower competing with the rich liquid tones of a Baltimore oriole.

The idyllic sounds bore a heavy contrast to what I'd witnessed at the reception. Chase had objected and struggled, so Henderson had summoned a uniformed Wanda, who must have been waiting outside during the service and reception. Between the two of them they got Chase handcuffed and walked him out to the accompaniment of several dozen silent stares. The silence hadn't lasted long, turning to murmured commentary among those who remained, some shocked by what they'd seen, some sounding satisfied.

We'd stopped by my store on our way home so I could change into jeans and grab a scarf in case the temperature dropped later on. When we'd arrived at Abe's, he had offered a sumptuous summer meal of grilled chicken, potato salad, and coleslaw. We hadn't spoken of the murders throughout dinner, but I thought he'd want to know what happened.

With only a few bites left on my plate, I began. "So Detective Henderson was at the reception. She arrested Chase for Pia's murder."

Roberto nodded, and Maria crossed herself.

Abe set his fork down. "Impressive news. How'd he take it?"

"He was furious, that's how. I wouldn't be surprised if he got a second count of resisting arrest. It took both Henderson and Wanda to get him handcuffed and out of there."

Roberto leaned forward. "Robbie, do you think she was correct, the detective? Do you think this man killed Pia?"

I gazed back at him. "I think it's possible. He wanted to run for senator in our national government. Pia was probably threatening him that she would tell the public of his affair with her."

"Maybe he should have thought of that before starting the relationship," Abe muttered, shaking his head.

"I know by now the police have to have actual evidence before they make an arrest," I said. "I don't think I told any of you that Adele talked to Gail, Chase's wife." I described the tracker the wife had put on Chase's car, and that I'd told the detective it was there. "So maybe they checked the tracker's software and found Chase had driven to Beanblossom in the night and then came back to my place." I shuddered. "I hate that a killer might have been staying upstairs."

Roberto murmured in Italian to Maria.

Her nostrils flared. "He is bad man, this Chase."

Abe drummed his fingers on the table. "Detective Henderson didn't also arrest him for Sue's murder?"

"No. The only name she said was Pia Bianchi." So who had killed Sue? Beth had left my B&B in a hurry, looking very much the guilty party. Was it her? Isaac during his time incommunicado? Glen himself? Or maybe Henderson suspected Chase also killed Sue but didn't have enough evidence to arrest him for a second murder. She could be hoping he'd confess while he was in custody.

The conversation turned to the bluegrass festival as we finished our dinners, and then to Roberto and Maria's return home tomorrow. Abe rose to clear the plates. Maria started to stand, but Abe waved her down.

"I got this," he said. "You are my guests."

"Okay, but you come visit us soon," Maria demanded in reply.

Abe raised an eyebrow at me. "Sounds like we should make a plan, Robbie." He smiled, dimple and all.

Travel to Italy with him? What a delightful thought. "You'll love it there," I answered.

As he headed into the kitchen with the plates, I heard my phone vibrating in my purse and excused myself to check the text. *Uh-oh.* Detective Henderson had a search warrant for Chase's room and needed to get in.

I turned away from my father and Maria and

called the detective. "I'm not home at the moment, but I should be able to get there in half an hour. Does that work for you?"

"Thank you, Ms. Jordan. I'll tell my team. I won't be with them, but they'll be in uniform and have appropriate identification." She rung off.

I stashed my phone, loaded my arms with the serving dishes, and followed Abe into the kitchen. "I'm going to need to run home for a few minutes in half an hour," I told him. "The detective has a search warrant for Chase's room."

"Interesting. Do you think she'll find anything?"

"I have no idea. But she must think they will." I found the drawer that held plastic storage containers. "Abe, do you know Ed and Beth, the couple who was staying in my B&B? She's a clogger and he's a fiddler."

He shut off the water in the sink and turned to me, wiping his hands on a red towel. "Ed Molina? And what's her last name, Fender or something?"

"Ferguson."

"I met them at a meeting for the festival performers. She's, um, kind of strange."

"Strange how?" I asked.

"She seems to hold a grudge for a long time. She was talking about some woman who had wronged her, and she used those exact words. Like she was in a country-western song or something. Have you ever heard anybody actually say, 'He wronged me?'"

I laughed. "Come to think of it, no. Who was the woman?"

"Somebody who had cheated her of money, I think." *Pia.* "Was Pia at the meeting?"

"Now that you mention it, she wasn't. Molina's a good dude," Abe went on. "Great fiddler. Why did you ask about him and Beth?"

I told him they'd left abruptly two days before they were scheduled to.

"That's funny." Abe pulled on his ear, as he often did while he was thinking. "I could have sworn they're on the program tonight."

"Maybe they are, but decided to drive home afterward."

"We could go the festival and catch their number." He glanced at the little analog clock in the stove, an appliance that looked almost as old as the house. "We have plenty of time to have dessert and still get over there. It's only seven. Roberto and Maria could come if they want. What do you think?"

"Sounds like fun. Maybe I can get my keys back from Ed. We can swing by the store on the way and let the detective's team in. Why don't you ask Roberto and Maria?"

After he left the room, I put away the leftovers and rinsed the serving dishes. Something about Chase being arrested didn't sit right with me. He had motive and means to kill Pia, certainly, and he'd acted suspiciously a few times, but was he really the murderer? And Sue's death? Did the detective have somebody else in mind for that? Was it, in fact, a copycat killing?

Chapter Forty

The four of us were finally seated in the audience of folding chairs and picnic cloths in front of the main stage. When we'd stopped by the store, the team had also showed me a search warrant for Beth's and Ed's room, so I had unlocked both the Sapphire and the Emerald guest rooms. The team leader didn't explain why they were searching Beth's room, but it sure comported with my guests' speedy and secretive premature departure.

Once we'd arrived at the music park, we'd had to walk forever from the outer reaches of the parking area. It was Friday night, after all, and the last weekend of the festival. We claimed spots in the viewing area, then Abe strode off in search of drinks. Recorded music by Bill Monroe and his Blue Grass Boys played over the loudspeakers as one group moved off the stage and another bustled around setting up. Two stagehands in black T-shirts and jeans adjusted microphones and handed each musician a bottle of water. Somebody must have taken over Sue's job, because things seemed to be running as smoothly as they had while she was alive and at the helm.

Roberto and Maria looked happy, sitting holding hands. He tapped his foot to the music as she swayed side to side in her chair. I gazed around the crowd. My eyes stopped at what looked like Beth leaning against a tree at the side, arms crossed, looking toward the stage.

"I'll be back in a minute," I told my father.

"Okay." He smiled and squeezed my hand.

I made my way through the audience until I reached her. "How's it going, Beth?" I kept my tone light, smiling.

She turned her head. She didn't smile back. "Hey there, Robbie."

"Are you performing tonight?"

She nodded. Her fingers drummed a fast beat on her arm, not in time to the music.

"So I was emptying wastebaskets in all the rooms today. It looked like you guys checked out early. Why didn't you tell me you were going to leave?"

She shrugged, gazing at the stage. "Ed wanted to."

"I still have to charge him for the whole time, you know. I had to turn away customers who wanted a room for the weekend."

"He can afford it."

"I need your keys back, too. The checkout procedure is posted in all the rooms."

"I lost my key. You'll have to ask him for his." The musicians onstage were tuning up. "I have to go."

She turned her back on me and wove through the people standing on the periphery until I lost sight of her. I sighed and swore under my breath. I was going to have to revise my procedure for checking out, and make it mandatory. I should also put a fee in place for lost keys.

I caught a glimpse of Wanda strolling along the edges of the audience. She wasn't in uniform but with her hands clasped behind her back and her eyes surveying the crowd, it looked like she was working, anyway. I headed her way.

"You're a bluegrass fan, Wanda?" I asked from a foot behind her.

She whirled, her hand going to her waist as if reaching for the gun she normally wore there. "You startled me, Robbie." Her out-of-uniform outfit tonight was denim capris topped by a snug blue festival T-shirt. It had *Bluegrass* emblazoned across the top. Under the word was a drawing of a banjo, fiddle, and guitar all leaning against an upright bass. Below the instruments I read, *and Everything Else.* I'd never seen Wanda's hair loose. Tonight it fell in strawberry-blond soft waves. In fact her entire appearance was way softer than usual.

I understood. If I were a female officer of the law, I wouldn't want to look soft on the job, either. But tonight Wanda fit right in.

"Sorry I startled you." What kind of detective-in-training lets herself be sneaked up on? "Detective Henderson arresting Chase Broward right there at Pia's memorial reception was kind of a shock."

Her lip curled. "I suppose. That man is slick. I don't trust him any farther than I can throw the Pope."

I snorted at the phrase. "How often do you throw the Pope?"

"You know what I mean. Anyhoo, he couldn't argue with the facts of that there tracker his wife attached to his vehicle. But you know what he told us?"

I shook my head.

"Said he did drive to a rendevoose with the victim, but that she was already a goner." She rhymed *rendezvous* with *hen caboose*.

"Really?"

"You better believe it. Told us he spied that other guest of yours, the dancer, running away from the scene."

My eyes went wide. "Beth?"

"Yupperooney. Ms. Elizabeth Ferguson herself."

"Did you believe him? What if he's lying?"

"Anne couldn't do much about it either way." Wanda's eyes kept scanning the crowd. "The man lawyered up and posted bail. He might could be here tonight. That's why I'm in attendance incognito. Keeping an eye out for him."

As if Wanda in civvies could ever pass as incognito. To music fans from out of town, maybe, but not to anyone who'd ever met her.

"And Beth?" I asked. "Did Henderson arrest her instead?"

"Gotta find her, first. She's not answering her phone and neither is Mr. Molina. But the evidence isn't there for an arrest, not yet."

"She's here. I talked with her a few minutes ago."

"Really? Thanks for the intel."

Wanda was being super forthcoming. What else could I learn from her? "Did Henderson let Isaac Rowling go?"

"Had to. Same problem. Nothing concrete to pin on the man."

"Too bad." I thought for a moment. "When Henderson arrested Chase, she only mentioned Pia's name. So she doesn't think he also killed Sue?"

"That's a stumper, all right. So far we got diddly-squat to connect the Berry murder with Mr. Broward. Zip. Nada." She shook her head. "Listen, I got to be continuing my surveillance here. You keep your eyes open, okay, Robbie?"

"Of course. Good luck."

From the loudspeakers came a man's voice. "Good evening." I turned toward the stage, as did Wanda. A man I didn't recognize stood in front of the band. I took a second look. Ed was in the group of musicians, holding his fiddle. Would Beth be clogging up there on the main stage?

"Many of you heard the second piece of sad news this week," the man onstage went on, and the crowd quieted. "Our wonderful, super good manager, Ms. Susan Berry, has passed away. We all mourn for her, and for her family. Her daughter, Paula, and her husband, Glen, would like a moment of your time, please."

Paula and Glen moved into the spotlight. He leaned into the microphone as the man stepped back.

"Thank you, all." His voice trembled like he was barely keeping it together. "My wife loved this kind of music, and we plan to start a scholarship in Sue's name for a young underprivileged musician to come here at no charge every year." He swallowed.

"For right now, we—" His voice broke and he bowed his head.

Paula put her arm around him and took over the microphone. She sniffed, but stood tall. "We have to help the authorities find the evil person who ended my mother's life." Unlike her father's, her voice was strong and clear. "Please, if you saw anything, witnessed anything suspicious, anything at all, please come forward and contact the sheriff's office over in Nashville. We need your help. Thank you."

Glen nodded mutely and let Paula guide him off the stage. It was brave of her to send out such a plea. I wondered if anyone would step forward. I also wondered if Glen's grief was as real as Paula's or was staged to cover guilt.

"Well, slap my head and call me silly." Wanda rubbed her chin. "Pretty sure them Berrys didn't clear their call for information with Anne. Wonder if we'll get any real info or only a bunch of calls from paranoid music fans seeing evil where it ain't. Anyhoo, I'm on the clock, so I best get moving. See you, Robbie." She resumed her walkabout.

The man onstage stepped forward again. "I second the plea. We have security measures in place, so rest assured you are safe here tonight and for the rest of the festival. But please do report to the police or even to a music park security guard anything the least bit unusual or suspicious. And now, let's give it up for the Moonshine Players!" He backed away, clapping, then hurried offstage.

The five musicians struck up a tune, playing in the fast precise style that characterized the genre. Ed was fiddling, and two men played a guitar and a banjo, while an upright bass and a mandolin were played by women. The banjo, bass, and mandolin players leaned into their mikes and sang in close harmony. All the musicians wore jeans with untucked shirts of various sorts except for the mandolin player, who paired red cowboy boots with a short denim skirt and a red plaid shirt, tails tied at her waist.

I started back to our chairs, but I kept my gaze on the stage. When the tune shifted, Beth clogged onstage to a round of enthusiastic clapping.

I glanced at Wanda over at the side of the audience. She'd definitely seen Beth up there, because she held a radio, or maybe a phone, in front of her mouth and was talking into it while keeping her gaze glued on the stage. Was she communicating with Henderson? I hadn't seen her tonight, but that didn't mean she wasn't here. Were we going to have a repeat of this afternoon, except with Beth arrested in public instead of Chase? No, Wanda had admitted they didn't have any hard evidence against Beth. What would evidence be? DNA on the banjo string? Something the killer had dropped in the bridge, maybe, or a fingerprint. But I didn't think they could extract a fingerprint from someone else's clothing or skin.

I shook my head. Finding evidence and arresting guilty parties was the detective's purview, not mine. I headed back to the chairs, to my father, my boyfriend, and hopefully a cold beer.

Chapter Forty-one

Beth clogged two numbers, then bowed and sashayed through one of the doors at the back of the stage. I must have been wrong that Henderson wanted to take Beth in for questioning. Or maybe she didn't want to make a spectacle out of it by plucking her off the stage. One spectacle per day was more than enough. I checked the area where I'd last seen Wanda, but she'd moved on. To make sure Beth didn't slip away? Could be.

I sat with Abe and the Italians, sipping my beer. They all seemed to be enjoying the music, as did the rest of the folks around us. My own enjoyment was tempered by thoughts of murder, but I tried to put suspects, motives, and the act of garroting out of my mind.

A man loomed large in front of me, blocking my view. When he didn't move on, I glanced up. Chase looked down at me. *Whoa.* Had I summoned him without meaning to? I didn't really believe in woo-woo stuff, but this was quite a coincidence. Or had he been following us? My insides felt like they were bathed in ice water, and my heart rate jumped into the aerobic range it normally only reached when I was riding hard up a hill.

"Evening, Robbie." He smiled but somehow it didn't reach his eyes. "I've been attempting to call you."

I swallowed. "Oh?" I slid my phone out of my bag. Yep, three missed calls. "Sorry. I turned the sound off for—" I stopped myself before I spoke of the memorial service. Surely he wouldn't want to be reminded of this afternoon. "I turned it down a few hours ago. Why were you calling?" I stood so I wasn't craning my neck. Abe stood, too, and laid a hand gently on my back. I was good at defending myself, and there were a couple hundred people around us, but it was always reassuring to have a strong and caring reinforcement nearby. Facing us was a man who'd very recently been arrested on a charge of murder, after all.

"I plan to return home earlier than expected," Chase said. "I'd like to extract my belongings from my room and turn in my key."

The police should have finished searching the room by now. "Your reservation was through Sunday, though, and I can't make a refund at this late date," I said in a firm tone. *Sheesh.* My first week as an innkeeper and two out of three rooms were defaulting on two nights. Thank goodness for credit cards.

"Not a problem. As you might have seen this afternoon, I've been falsely accused of wrongdoing." He lifted his chin. "And my last set here at the festival has been canceled by the management. Do you have an issue with me going over there now? I can leave my keys on the bureau in the room."

While the upstairs outside door locked itself when it closed, I wasn't particularly interested in him going onto the property when it was empty. "I'd be more comfortable if you came back tomorrow. Any time after seven in the morning when the store opens is fine." But what if he had prescription medications he couldn't do without? I'd have to leave the concert now, or we would all have to, since we'd driven together. Because no way was I getting a ride home from Chase Broward. I waited for him to offer objections.

After a moment's pause, he said, "Very well. I'll be back tomorrow."

"Why don't you give Robbie your keys now," Abe said.

Abe glanced at me for confirmation, and I gave a little nod. *Good idea. No, a great idea.* Even if I asked Chase not to go in tonight, he didn't have anything stopping him if I was out and he still held the keys.

Chase pressed his lips together, but apparently aspirants to the United States Senate shouldn't argue with logic, even if they didn't like it. He dug into his pocket and dropped the keys on their ring, which was identified by a green bead, onto my waiting palm.

"Thanks," I said. "See you in the morning." After he walked away, I squeezed Abe's hand and sank into my chair again. My core warmed again and my heart returned to a normal resting pulse, or close to it.

Abe sat, too. Roberto looked quizzical, but Maria had alarm written all over her face. They'd both seen the detective take Chase away in handcuffs this afternoon.

"It's nothing," I said. "I saw the deputy detective

and she told me Chase is out on bail." I watched Roberto to see if he knew the word, and he seemed to. He turned to Maria to explain.

"But he is still accused of the killing?" my father asked when he was finished translating.

"I think so," I said.

"In Italia, killers do not go free in this way." Roberto pressed his lips together and shook his head.

"It's the American way," Abe offered.

Roberto threw his hands up in *what can you do?* gesture. He drained the last sip of his beer and pushed up to standing. "I go to the men's room." He translated for his wife and set off between the chairs, murmuring, "*Scusa, scusa,*" to people he passed in front of.

"You have keys back from the man?" Maria asked haltingly. "And he go," she made a sweeping gesture.

"Thanks to Abe." I dangled the key ring in the air, then slid them into my bag. "Yes, he's gone."

"Good. I no like him." Maria wiped her hands off on each other a couple *of* times in the universal gesture indicating *finished, done with it*.

"Thanks, Abe," I said. "Really smart move to ask for the keys back."

"Glad I'm good for something." He laid his arm around my shoulders and stuck his legs out in front. His tennies were a florescent orange.

I laughed. "Those shoes are kind of blinding."

"You like them?" He lifted his right foot in the air and rotated it. "I know, they're bright. I haven't had a chance to get them dirty yet."

We settled in to watch the show. The group with Ed on the fiddle was still onstage. When they started a new piece, Beth emerged again and clogged onto center stage.

"Speaking of keys," I said to Abe, "I still need my keys back from Ed. Beth said she'd lost hers, but I'm not sure I believe her. Maybe I should go up there now and wait for them to be done."

"After the group finishes they'll surely be called back for an encore. You can go up then."

"Good idea." I watched until the number finished. The woman on the mandolin, who had been doing all the talking, thanked the audience and the band filed off. When the clapping and enthusiastic hoots continued, the group emerged again. Beth did, too.

I stood. "I'll be back."

"Want company?" Abe asked.

"No, you stay with Maria. I'll be in sight of hundreds of people." I made my way to the right hand side of the stage.

These musicians were really good at what they did. I couldn't believe how fast fingers were flying on the banjo and the mandolin, especially. Seen from so close up it was pretty impressive. Ed got the spotlight for a bit, and his fingers raced up and down as fast as his bow, with Beth's feet keeping up. Then it was over.

I'd seen steps leading up to the back of the stage on the right side but not on the left, so I positioned myself at the bottom of them. Four older gentlemen all in black suits, filed past me with their instruments and trotted up the stairs. The next group, no doubt. Someone scuffled a foot behind me and I turned to see Wanda.

"I bet I know who you're waiting for," I said. "Me, too."

"You won't interfere with the law, I trust?" she said.

Really, Wanda? "Of course not. I only want to get my keys back. Beth and Ed cleared out without checking out."

"That'll be fine, then." She stood with her feet apart and her elbows out in a classic tough guy stance that didn't match her outfit, pushing a fist into the palm of her other hand over and over.

The mandolin player emerged, and then Ed and Beth together. They were talking in low voices. Their expressions looked like they were arguing. When the couple reached the bottom of the stairs, Beth glanced up, catching sight of Wanda. The clogger's face morphed from disgruntled to panicked. She turned to reverse her steps, but the guitarist, the banjo player, and their instruments blocked the steps coming down, and the bassist and her bass were directly behind them. Beth and Ed had no choice but to move forward out of their way.

Wanda stepped toward them, all business. "Ms. Ferguson, Detective Henderson asked me to accompany you to the station. We have a few questions we need to ask you."

Beth wrapped her arms around herself, tight, and shook her head eyes wide. "I can't. I have to go. I—"

Wow. Quite the different reaction from the cool, disdainful Beth I'd talked to earlier. Now she looked terrified. Sweat beaded on her upper lip and I caught a whiff of fear.

Ed slung his own arm around her shoulders. "Of course we'll go. We have nothing to hide, right, babe?"

Even through her panic Beth looked like she'd tasted a moldy piece of bread at being called *babe.*

I stepped forward. "Could I get your keys back, Ed?" Might as well cushion it a little. "Beth said you guys checked out but forgot to leave the keys."

Ed shot Beth a quick glance, but not so quick I didn't notice. He knew she'd been lying.

"Of course." He dug in his messenger bag and handed me two key rings, both with a blue bead.

Yep, Beth had lied. "Thanks so much. As I told Beth, the full week's charge will appear on your bill."

"Fine, fine." He waved me away.

Wanda cleared her throat. "If you don't mind?" She extended her arm in a way that clearly indicated it didn't matter if they minded or not.

Chapter Forty-two

When I arrived back at our chairs, my father's was still empty. Maria, brow furrowed, kept turning and looking to her left in the direction he'd headed for the restroom. A while ago. *Huh?*

"Where's my father?" I asked Abe in a low voice. Nobody needed that much time to use the bathroom. Roberto was traveling outside his comfort zone, though, and maybe some American food he'd tried had disagreed with him. That very thing had happened to me when I visited Italy, and I'd had to spend more than a few minutes on the commode one day. "Did he go get more drinks?"

Abe shook his head. "He's not back from the head. I'll go look for him, since you're here now." Hiding his right hand with his left, he pointed at Maria and telegraphed a message I was pretty sure read, *She's worried.*

"Got it. Go." I sat and smiled at Maria, who was tapping her foot. "Do you like the music?"

"I like it. But Roberto? I worried."

"I'm sure it's fine. Abe went to look for him. Maybe he saw a friend."

"Friend Don?"

"Sure. Or someone else he met this week, or maybe somebody he knew when he was here before." I spoke as clearly as I could.

She nodded, but her remarkable eyebrows still drew together in the middle. The new group finished one song and started another. These men in their black suits and dress shirts presented a very different stage presence than the preceding band, as well as a slower, twangier style of playing and singing.

Still no Abe, still no Roberto. Now I was getting worried, too, plus I needed to get back and start food prep for tomorrow. I stood and scanned the area, but it was even more crowded than when we'd arrived an hour earlier. I sent Abe a text.

You OK? Can't find R?

No response. Why not? Where were they? Hanging out at the drinks booth? Corrine and Danna strolled toward us. I waved to get their attention.

"Well, slap my head and call me silly," Corrine said, using the same phrase Wanda had. "Howdy, there, Robbie. And this lovely lady might be?"

"Mom, I told you." Danna rolled her eyes in a younger-teen kind of reaction I rarely saw at the store. Probably because I was her boss, not her mother.

"Corrine, this is my father's wife, Maria Fracasso. Maria, meet Corrine Beedle. She's Danna's mother and the mayor of South Lick." I thought hard. Had I learned the word for mayor? *Sindaco.* Or was it *sindaca* if the mayor was a woman?

Maria stood and pumped Corrine's hand. "*Sindaco.* I pleased to meet you. Danna, she is good girl. And very good cook."

Danna blushed.

"Maria, welcome to Indiana," Corrine said. She had dressed down—for Corrine—in a festival T-shirt tied in an off-center knot at her waist and tight jeans tucked into tooled red cowboy boots with a good-sized heel on them.

"Are you playing tonight, Corrine?" I asked.

"No, us ladies had our fill the other evening. I'm in the audience tonight, me and my girl."

"Isaac's not with you?" I asked Danna.

"No. He was . . . uh"—she glanced at her mom—"busy. He was busy."

Busy? Was he still being questioned at the station? No, Wanda had said they'd had to let him go. I hoped he wasn't having another flare-up.

Corrine turned to Maria. "And where is your hand-some husband? I want to meet him, too."

Maria's face fell and she turned to me to explain.

"Roberto went to the men's room a while ago," I explained. "He hasn't come back. Abe went off a little while ago to find him, but he's not back, either, as you can see."

Corrine listened intently. For all her big hair and southern accent, she was one sharp lady. "We got one or two bad guys still at large," she murmured to me. "I heared the sheriff was obliged to let Chase Broward loose. Think you should oughta get some help from the authorities to find your father and your man?"

I stared at her. The thought of the murderer going after *Babbo* or Abe roiled my stomach. "Really?"

The mayor thought for a moment, then spoke normally. "Tell you what. Danna, darlin', why don't you set with Ms. Fracasso a couple few minutes? Robbie and me are going to hunt us up a couple men." She kept her tone light.

"Cool. I'm sure you'll find them," Danna said, plopping into my chair.

"Let's go, girlfriend." Corrine set out to the left, stopping once in a while to shake someone's hand or tweak a child's cheek. Her constituents were everywhere.

I followed in her considerable wake, all my senses alert. I heard what sounded like angry men's voices to my right and whipped my head in that direction, but it was only a couple of dudes in cowboy hats arguing the merits of Cubs versus Cards. We passed the beer booth, where four women behind the table were filling big plastic cups with draft beer or uncapping beer bottles as fast as they could. I scanned for my guys. No Abe. No Roberto.

As I was searching from side to side while walking, trying to keep up with Corrine, I heard a soft, "Oof." I'd just walked straight into Paula Berry.

"I'm sorry, Paula. I wasn't looking where I was going." Corrine hadn't noticed. "Corrine, hang on," I called.

But over the buzz of the crowd and the amplified

music, she must not have heard me. She disappeared into the scrum of bluegrass fans.

I focused on Paula again, who held a bottle of beer in each hand. "I'm surprised to see you here." I kept my voice gentle for her. "Is Glen around?"

"Daddy said he had to leave. I hooked up with my friend. Mom loved this music so much, I wanted to lose myself in it for a while." Her eyes were red-rimmed and a little bloodshot, too, and she swayed a bit.

I wondered how many beers she'd already downed. "You're not driving, right?"

"No, my friend is, and the baby is with my friend's hubby, who adores children." She peered into my face. "I don't think Daddy really loved Mom. Did you know that?"

Interesting. Why would she say such a thing? "I'm sure he did, Paula."

She shook her head sorrowfully. "No. Maybe a long time ago he did. Not anymore. I don't think he liked her very much, either." A dainty hiccup slipped out. She giggled and lifted a hand to cover her mouth. "Excuse me." She glanced at her hand as if surprised to find a bottle in it, and one in the other hand, too. "I have to go give my friend her beer. Thanks for listening to me, Robbie." She leaned in and gave my cheek a beery kiss.

"You take care, now." I watched her weave into the crowd. It wouldn't hurt for her to lose her sorrow in a couple of beers, as long as she wasn't driving. I wondered where Glen had gone. Home? Or was he still on the festival grounds? Was Isaac lurking here, too? And had Chase really left?

The noise all around pressed in until I couldn't stand it. I covered my ears with my hands, but I couldn't just stand here like one of the three wise monkeys.

I checked my phone. The time was nine-ten. I decided if I didn't find the guys by nine-twenty, I was calling it in. I pushed on in the direction I thought Corrine had gone. There. I finally spotted a big red RESTROOMS sign. This was the one on the opposite side of the park from the one where I'd seen the clogging the other night. I hurried toward it, arriving at a wide building with a gently sloping ramp up to both ends. I didn't see Corrine anywhere. I couldn't very well go inside the door labeled MEN and see if Abe and my father were in there. I glanced into the women's side and called out Corrine's name but no one answered. I stooped down and checked for feet in the stalls. Nobody was in here.

I made my way out and circled behind the building nestled into the edge of the woods. All the trees were in full leaf and the underbrush was thick with saplings and years' worth of fallen leaves. A breeze rustled the leaves with a scratching sound as a small animal scurried away. A crow cawed from behind me, making me jump, then it beat its wings with a rustle, flying into the woods.

When I spied a beaten down path between the trees, a path winding into the darkness, I had a strong urge to follow it. Something told me Abe and *Babbo* were in there somewhere, having been abducted or worse by a murderer.

But Nancy Drew I was not, nor Kinsey Millhone, either. I pulled out my phone. I ought to call Detective Anne Henderson. But would she laugh at me and say they had to let twenty-four hours pass before filing a missing persons report? I shook my head and pressed Buck's number. He wouldn't laugh.

Chapter Forty-three

Buck didn't laugh, but he didn't say he'd be right there, either.

"So your papa and your boyfriend are lost at the bluegrass festival?" he asked, incredulity creeping into his voice. "You sure they didn't head off to one of the other stages?"

True, there were three or four other stages, plus the tailgate jam sessions that popped up all over the place. I sighed. "Okay, I'll go check everywhere else. But Buck, listen to me. All the murder suspects except Beth Ferguson are out here somewhere. I mean, they aren't locked up. What if—"

"What if the killer knows you was snooping around like you're not sposta be doing, and abducted your father to get back at you? Mr. Fracasso is a growed man. Looked strong enough when I met him. You think he couldn't defend himself?"

"But what if the killer has a gun or something?" I heard my voice rise with impatience. "What if Abe is hurt, too?" I stared at the path. I could swear I saw something purple hanging from a bush.

"Robbie, calm down now. Tell you what. I'll alert Wanda. I know she was working the festival tonight."

"That's not going to work. She took Beth in for questioning an hour ago." I kept staring into the woods, which were getting darker by the minute now the sun had finally set. I couldn't see the purple color any more. I shivered.

"All righty then. I'll put my uniform back on and come down there. It's the wife's birthday and we was finishing a nice dinner. Candles and all whatnot. But I'll help you."

How thoughtless could I be, calling him on a Friday night? "I'm sorry. Never mind. Don't leave your nice dinner."

"The wife would be most appreciative if I stayed put. But listen up. They've got to have security guards around the festival. Find one. They'll help you out. Maybe they can even make a announcement, you know, from up on the stage or somewheres."

"Good idea. I'm sorry I bothered you, Buck. Please tell your wife happy birthday from me."

"I will, soon's I hang up. You stay safe, now."

"Thanks." I disconnected the call. This evening was going to all heck in handbasket, as Adele would say. I wished we'd never come to the festival. We could have stayed at Abe's house, comfortable and safe, having coffee or an after-dinner drink, getting some last visiting in before my visitors left tomorrow. Instead, here I was in the dark with a few thousand strangers. I was separated from Roberto and Abe, two of the three people I loved most in the world, Adele being the third. I also didn't know where Corrine had gone. I hoped I could find my way back to Maria and Danna. I should touch base with them before hunting down a security guard. Except I didn't want to arrive empty-handed, so to speak. I'd seen how worried Maria was.

My phone dinged with an incoming text. Abe? I checked it. Not from Abe, but from Danna. Mom's back here. Where are u?

Whew. At least Corrine hadn't gone missing, too.

I tapped in a return message. At restrooms. Going to find security guard for help.

Ding.

Hurry. Maria about to lose it.

I turned to go find a guard. And turned back. I had to at least take a look at the opening. I wouldn't go any farther alone. I hit the flashlight app on my phone and moved toward the path, scanning it back and forth as I went.

The light fell on purple. My heart thudded. It had to be Abe's handkerchief. I rushed toward the spot a few yards away . . . and tripped on a root. The phone went flying. I crashed onto my right knee before my hands hit the ground. I swore out loud. Then I cursed myself silently. What if Abe and Roberto had been attacked and now the bad guy knew where I was, too?

Chapter Forty-four

I carefully pushed up to standing, dusting myself off, testing my knee. All systems were go, except for my phone. I peered into the underbrush. A glimmer of light peeked out at me. I retrieved it and dusted it off, too. No cracks, and still operational thanks to the military-grade rubber case which protected it from a klutzy owner. I heaved a sigh of relief worthy of a Tour de France cyclist at the finish line.

I wanted to shout Abe's name, and my father's, too. Instead, I gave up on the purple handkerchief and hurried around to the front of the building. Where was I going to find a guard? I remembered where we'd entered the park. There had to be an office of some kind there. But the entrance was on the opposite side from where I stood. Shouldn't guards be patrolling among us? Guarding the periphery? Making sure people didn't get drunk and into fights? Although as a rule, bluegrass fans were a pretty congenial group.

Wait. *Drunk.* There had to be a guard near the beer booth to police underage drinking if nothing else. I made my feet of lead move until I was walking normally. I hadn't even reached the beer booth when I saw a bulky someone heading my way wearing the bright yellow polo shirt of the park staff. I hurried to meet him.

"Excuse me, sir." I waved at him to catch his attention.

"Can I help you, miss?" He was as tall as Buck but probably weighed half again as much. The weight looked like it was all muscle, with his biceps straining at the sleeves. BCMP SECURITY was embroidered on his shirt and he wore a name badge that read LONNIE. On his belt hung a walkie-talkie.

I opened my mouth. What was I going to tell him? I should keep it simple. "My father has gone missing here somewhere. He's visiting from Italy, and I'm a bit worried about him."

Lonnie ushered me to the side of the walkway, which was full of people moving in each direction, many carrying instruments, some moseying, some walking briskly to the rhythm coming from loudspeakers. One young couple, hand in hand, danced to the music as they walked.

The guard cocked his head. To his credit he didn't look at me like I was nuts. "Does your pa have dementia?"

I glanced again at his eyes, which were a deep blue. "No, not at all. He's a professor, and not so old. Maybe sixty, tops. And he speaks English pretty well, too. But maybe he got, um, turned around or something."

"What is your name, and your father's?"

"I'm Robbie Jordan and he's Roberto Fracasso."

"Lonnie Dinnsen," He took a closer look. "You the Miz Jordan who runs that really tasty breakfast joint? I hear about you all over the place."

"I own and run Pans 'N Pancakes in South Lick, yes. We offer breakfast, lunch, and vintage kitchenware."

He nodded knowingly. "And you're some kind of private detective, too, am I right?"

"No, not really."

"Say, what about this week, huh? Not one but two murders." He whistled. "One of 'em our own Miz Berry, too. It's a crying shame, that's what it is."

"Those murders are why I'm worried for my father, Lonnie." Since he'd broken the ice, so to speak, I might as well tell him the truth. "I've kind of been poking around, asking some questions, and I thought maybe the murderer," *or one of them,* "might have lured Roberto into a dangerous situation. To get back at me or lure me into the same danger."

"Huh."

"Yeah. On top of it, my boyfriend went to look for Roberto and now he hasn't come back, either, and he's not answering my texts. His name is Abe O'Neill."

"I'll see what I can do, Miz Jordan. First imma call festival headquarters and tell 'em to keep a lookout for your papa and for Mr. O'Neill, too."

"Can they make an announcement to have them meet me at the gate?"

"I don't see why not." He pulled out his walkie-talkie and turned up the sound.

At first all I heard was a bunch of static, and then Lonnie relayed my message.

"Roberto Fracasso, right?" he checked with me.

I nodded, even though he'd butchered the pronunciation, saying something like Ruhbirdo Frack-uh-so. He was so friendly and helpful I wanted to hug this guy.

He put the walkie-talkie back in its holder. "Okey-doke. They're gonna do it on each stage next chance they get." He narrowed his eyes. "You haven't told the police?"

"I called Buck Bird. He's the lieutenant over in South Lick where my store is. Buck suggested I find a security guard here."

"I know Buck. Good man. Anyways, we're in county jurisdiction here. It's not his territory." He pointed a finger at me. "We'll find your menfolk, little lady. Don't you worry about a thing."

Little lady? I felt my ire rising at the term but I tamped it down. I needed the guard's help. As for not worrying? Easier said than done, big guy.

"Do you have a flashlight?" I asked Lonnie.

"Sure, I got me a light." He pulled a good-sized flashlight out of his back pocket.

"I'd really like it if you'd come with me to check something out. I saw a path going into the woods behind the building there." I pointed.

"I know that path. It leads out to Toothpick Hill Road eventually, but it goes through the woods quite a piece first. What do you need checked out?"

"I might have seen my boyfriend's handkerchief on a bush. I was thinking maybe he went on the path looking for Roberto. My father."

Lonnie cocked his head as if evaluating if I was a nut job or not, then finally nodded. "I'll come with you. Lemme radio in my position first." He clicked on his walkie-talkie and conveyed his plan. A static-filled reply I couldn't understand came back.

I glanced at my phone. No new texts, and the time was nine-forty already. I tapped my leg in a fast rhythm. *Let's go, already.*

"Ten four," Lonnie added before turning the volume down again. "Cleared to proceed."

We made our way around to the back of the rest-rooms. In the distance I heard a cheer go up from the audience at the amphitheater. Some big name must have come onstage. Lonnie clicked on his light after the building blocked most of the illumination from the festival. He scanned the flashlight beam back and forth until it landed on the opening in the woods. "You with me?" he asked.

"I'm right behind you. If you see a purple hand-kerchief, stop. I think it was on the left a little ways in."

Sure enough, he hadn't taken two steps in when he halted. The light shone full on Abe's handkerchief, still partly folded, where it was snagged on the bare branch of a young shagbark hickory. I peered around Lonnie's side.

"It's Abe's. See? He even gets them monogrammed." I pointed to the initials *AJO* in a corner of the hanky. Abraham James O'Neill. Had he left it there on pur-pose as a signpost? Had he left it because he was in trouble or had lost his phone, or had he dropped it accidentally while he went looking for my father?

"Fancy. I think we'll leave it there, if you don't

mind, miss." He pulled out a phone and snapped a picture of the handkerchief. "Could be evidence."

Evidence. "Okay." I swallowed down the tremble in my voice. "Can we keep going?"

He looked at me and frowned. "I'm not so sure you should be accompanying me. Being that you're a civilian and all."

"Please?" I hated how plaintive I sounded. I cleared my throat and tried again. "I know both of them, and they know my voice. Plus, you should have company."

He scrunched one eye closed, peering at me with the other like I'd made a ludicrous suggestion. He opened his eye again. "Not sure how a little bit of a thing like you is going to help me. But you win. Come along."

He had a point, I had to admit. I was simply glad he was letting me go with him. If he'd been Buck, or worse, Detective Henderson, I was pretty sure I would have been told in no uncertain terms to go back to my seat and wait. Waiting is not one of my superpowers.

Lonnie shone the light on the ground ahead and set out with careful steps, treading with amazing silence for such a big man. I followed.

We walked quietly for what seemed like forever. I pulled out my phone to check the time. Only five minutes had actually elapsed. Still no text from Abe. My hands felt numb, distant, and I almost dropped the phone before I slid it into my pocket.

Lonnie threw an arm out to the side and stopped so abruptly I ran into his bulk.

"Sorry," I whispered.

He twisted to look at me and held a finger to his lips. The kindly smiling guard was gone, replaced by an all-business watchman. He cupped a hand to his ear.

I did, too. I caught a faint low sound. Not the rustle of leaves or the scrabbling of a small woods mammal. It was a human sound. A moan.

Chapter Forty-five

I tugged at Lonnie's sleeve. He nodded, holding up a hand in a *Stop* gesture. We both stood stock-still, listening. *There.* Another moan, fainter this time. Coming from ahead. Lonnie began to move forward, slowly, carefully. I followed, equally carefully. The darkness smelled damp, of pine needles and leaf mold.

He switched the light to a red beam. It still lit up the path but wasn't as bright as the brilliant white in the dark. I kept my gaze on the circle of red as we walked with excruciatingly slow steps. It was like gliding through a dream. Or rather, a nightmare.

The light moved onto an orange athletic shoe. A fluorescent orange tennie. I inhaled sharply. In a second Lonnie had illuminated Abe lying on his side, one arm flung up over his ear as if fending off a blow.

My heart was in my throat, beating like a hurricane. I could hardly swallow. My eyes filled. I brought my hand to my mouth.

Lonnie handed me the light and knelt. I shone

the light on Abe's head as Lonnie checked his neck for a pulse. He nodded and gave me a thumbs-up.

Abe was alive. But unconscious. He moaned and shifted his legs.

I knelt on his other side, laying my hand on his cheek. "I'm here, Abe," I whispered.

His eyes fluttered open but remained half lidded. "Wha . . ." he murmured.

"It's okay," I responded in kind, stroking his face.

Lonnie again put his finger to his lips. Questions flooded my brain. Where was Roberto? Who had done this to Abe, and what had they done? Where was the criminal now? Lurking nearby? Driving Roberto somewhere?

Abe's eyes came all the way open. He glanced from me to Lonnie and back. His eyes went wider. He struggled to sit up. Lonnie put his thick arm behind Abe's shoulders and helped him. Abe winced. He swore in a low raspy voice.

"What happened?" I asked in a whisper.

"Searched everywhere," he whispered back. "Saw the path. Thought Roberto might have gone this way. Came to find him. Thought I saw a clearing ahead. Heard a sound. Then, I don't know."

"Where are you hurt?" I asked.

He felt the back of his head. When he brought his hand back, the red light showed a darker red blotch. "I guess somebody knocked me out."

My eyes had adjusted enough to see Lonnie frowning. I wanted to do the same but didn't want to worry Abe. What should we do now? Keep looking for Roberto? He might be similarly knocked out just ahead. Or worse. I almost lost it picturing him in distress. But I didn't want to leave Abe here. He needed medical attention. From the look on Lonnie's face, I expected he was beset with the same questions.

Abe made a few of my worries moot. He extended a hand to Lonnie. "Help me up, man."

Lonnie reached his meaty hand to Abe, who stood.

"We have to find Roberto," Abe said.

"Are you okay?" I asked him, rubbing his arm, searching his face.

"I can see fine." He extended his arms to the side and stood still for a moment. "I'm not off balance. Head hurts a little, but not bad. I'm not concussed. Scalp wounds bleed a lot. I'll have a goose egg tomorrow, but I'm good to keep going."

He'd been a medic in the military some years ago, a piece of his past I occasionally spaced out on, and he knew how to assess his own well-being. He extended his hand to Lonnie.

"Abe O'Neill."

The guard shook his hand. "Lonnie Dinnsen. Security guard for the park."

"Can you sweep the ground with your light?" Abe asked. "I dropped mine."

I was getting antsy to keep going toward my father, but conceded two lights would be better than one. Using the light app on my phone burned battery like nobody's business, and my charge was already running low.

A text came in from Danna. I checked it as the guys searched for the flashlight.

What's happening? she'd written.

"There," Abe said, pointing to a small blue cylinder.

He picked it up and pressed the end. For such a tiny device, it had a superstrong light.

"Let's go," Lonnie murmured. "I'll lead. One of you bring up the rear."

Abe pointed to his chest. I nodded and pocketed my phone again. I didn't have time to answer Danna. I was glad my complete attention was on the path, because in a few yards it did widen into a clearing. As Lonnie ran his light along the perimeter on the left and Abe on the right, I let out an involuntary yelp. Abe's light had caught the shine on Roberto's distinctly Italian leather shoes.

Let Babbo *be alive. Please let him be alive.*

Chapter Forty-six

I rushed to my father where he sat with his back to a tree on the periphery of the clearing. Facing the woods, his legs were extended, his hands behind his back. His head didn't loll, though. He held it erect and his dark eyebrows went way up when he saw me. A piece of gray duct tape covered his mouth. A matching piece bound his ankles together.

He made sounds in his throat like he was trying to talk. It was like listening underwater—I couldn't understand what he was saying. It sounded desperate. Who had done this to him? Were they still around? Watching? Hair stood up on my arms and the nape of my neck.

I knelt in front of him. "I'm going to take the tape off," I whispered with a shaking voice. "It'll hurt." I licked my suddenly dry lips.

He nodded. My hands were sweating as I tried to peel back a corner to get a grip on it. Abe made it to my side and stood behind me, shining his light down on my task. *Babbo's* eyes widened to saucers and he shook his head so hard I lost my hold on the tape.

He croaked out a rising and falling sound of urgency, his gaze focused on Abe.

A rustle sounded from the woods and I glanced up. Chase Broward loomed behind Abe. Where had he come from?

"Watch out!" I cried, but I was too late.

He looped a wire around Abe's neck. Chase's hands pulled it tighter. Abe's eyes bugged out. The pool of light hit his foot but he didn't drop the flash. He clutched at Chase's forearm with his other hand, trying to pull it away.

Over Abe's shoulder Chase glared at me with a burning fury. "Damn snoop. You ruined everything. I was all set. Pia was out of the way. I could focus on my campaign. Until you started poking around, that is. I know you were asking questions. I know you were in my room."

The card. He'd noticed I'd never put the card back in his door.

Chase tugged on the wire. Abe made a gurgling sound.

"Lonnie!" I yelled.

Abe swung the little light up and over his shoulder into Chase's eye. Chase screamed. Lonnie appeared behind him. He grabbed Chase by both arms, yanked him away from Abe, and then wrestled him to the ground.

Abe fell to his knees, the wire still around his neck. His eyes implored me. In one movement I scooted next to him. Behind his head the ends of the wire were fastened to two short sticks of wood Chase had twisted the wire with. I unwound as fast as I could.

The wire fell away from Abe's throat onto the ground. He brought one hand to his neck.

"Did it cut you?" I asked, the words rushing out.

He brought his hand away and rubbed bloody fingers against his palm. "A little," he croaked. "Stings. Not too bad." He poked his hand into each of his back pockets.

"If you're looking for your handkerchief, it's on a bush back at the start of the path. We saw it there. But here." I extended the clean white hanky I often stuck in my own pocket. "Let's put this on the cut and then I'll use my scarf to hold it on." I unwound my jewel-colored turquoise silk scarf.

Abe nodded. I stretched the hanky out on the diagonal and laid it on the thin red line. I drew the scarf over the handkerchief and around his neck as gently as I could, tucking the ends into his shirt. He had given me the scarf a few months ago. I couldn't think of a better use of it.

"Robbie, see if the duct tape is still around," Lonnie called. Chase lay struggling facedown. Lonnie had one knee on his back and our attacker's hands secured in both of his. "My light is behind you."

I found his light lying a couple yards away. I switched it to white and scanned the area around Roberto. I took a moment to tell my father, "Just a minute, okay? I'll get the tape off you."

He tilted his head to the left a couple times.

"The tape is over there?" I asked.

"I can see it." Abe pointed.

I stepped over my father's legs and found the roll of wide gray tape. I gingerly extended it to Lonnie, being careful to stay clear of Chase's kicking legs, although he didn't have a chance with Lonnie's bulk on top of him.

Finally, I got back to my father and knelt once again. "Ready?"

He nodded, and I peeled back the tape.

He winced, but "Thank you, daughter," were his first words.

I struggled to keep my overflowing emotions from doing exactly that. My father easily could have been lying here garroted and dying instead of being tied up and muzzled.

"My hands, also." He leaned forward so I could see his bound wrists.

Between the darkness and my awkward position, I had trouble finding the edge of the tape. Abe, his multi-tool knife out and ready, gently shouldered me aside.

"Let me." He carefully slit the tape around Roberto's wrists and did the same to his ankles. Meanwhile, Lonnie had accomplished the reverse with Chase, securing his hands behind his back and taping his ankles together.

Lonnie stood, dusting off his hands. He took two steps and squatted in front of Roberto. "You all right, sir?"

"I am, thanks to my rescuers."

"O'Neill?" Lonnie checked with Abe.

"I'll be fine. It's a surface wound. Nothing that won't heal."

"Good," Lonnie said. "Now, I need to turn this clown over to the county authorities, and I can't leave him here unattended." He took out his walkie-talkie and turned it up. "Dinnsen here. Please acknowledge." But all he got back was static. He looked at the three of us clustered on the ground. "I'm out of range."

I pulled out my phone. "You can use my cell."

"Perfect."

I stood. "I have Detective Henderson's number. Do you want it?" I swiped it to the home screen and handed it to Lonnie.

"I need to call park headquarters first." He thumbed in the number with agility despite how thick his fingers were.

Abe stood, too, and extended a hand to Roberto, helping him up. We moved into the clearing. I wanted to get as far away from Chase as I could. As Lonnie turned his back slightly to speak, a nearly full moon peeked over the tops of the trees and lit up the clearing. I half expected fairies to appear and dance in the silver-splashed circle to celebrate our escape from danger.

Chapter Forty-seven

Within what seemed like minutes two all-terrain vehicles bumped toward us, lights on high. The drivers of the ATVs screeching to a halt in the clearing were park employees, wearing shirts similar to Lonnie's. A sheriff's sport utility vehicle followed, scraping branches on both sides as it barely made it along the path. Wanda and Detective Henderson climbed out of the SUV after it stopped.

Lonnie stepped forward. "Broward's over there"— he pointed with his thumb—"and not all that happy with the situation. Fair warning."

I had filled Lonnie in on who Chase was while we'd waited. I'd also texted Danna to say we were all together and safe, and to tell Maria we'd see her soon. I wanted to tell her Isaac was off the hook for Pia's murder, but decided to save it for later.

Henderson stepped forward and shook Lonnie's hand. "Nice work, Mr. Dinnsen."

"It was a group effort, believe me, ma'am."

"Ms. Jordan, you folks all right?" Henderson asked.

"Abe needs to be looked at," I said.

Abe nodded, gingerly patting his throat. "Wire cut needs cleaning," he croaked, his voice not back to normal. "And Broward managed to crack me on the head, too. None of it is urgent."

"Mr. Fracasso?" she asked, gazing at my father.

"No problems, thank you," he answered.

The detective and Wanda headed for Chase. Lonnie followed.

A woman on one of the ATVs spoke up. "We can give y'all a ride back to the park. But we can each take only one."

"Abe, you should go," I said.

"No, I'm staying with you and Roberto."

"*Babbo*, you take a ride," I urged. "We'll meet you back there."

"No. I stay, also."

"If I don't have any takers, the least I can do is go slow in front of you all to light the way," the park employee said.

"Sounds good," I said. "Thanks."

Henderson and Wanda emerged from the woods with Chase hobbling between them, duct tape straining between his ankles. Venomous words spewed from his mouth when he saw me.

"Now, now, Broward. Let's be polite," Wanda scolded. She opened the back door of the SUV and ushered him in, protecting his head from the top of the doorway. A Plexiglas window divided front seat from back, and a wire mesh sectioned off the rear from the molded plastic backseat. Wanda thudded the door shut, turning back to the rest of us.

"I have questions for the four of you, as you might

imagine," Henderson began. "Mr. Dinnsen, is there an office back at the park I can use?"

"Sure." He explained where it was, and the female ATV driver said she would lead the detective there.

"We're going to walk back," I said. "We have to get Maria. We'll be there as soon as we can."

"Where is Ms. Fracasso?" Henderson asked.

"Sitting with Danna Beedle and possibly Corrine in the main stage audience."

"I can take and bring her," Wanda offered.

"Thanks, but I think she'd be too nervous around a uniform."

Roberto nodded his agreement with my assessment.

"We won't be long," Abe said.

We stood back while Wanda turned the vehicle around. One of the ATVs led the way in front of the SUV, and the other set out slowly ahead of us four. The moonlight helped light our path, too.

"Roberto, how did you end up in the woods with Chase?" I asked.

"I was stupid. Mr. Broward came up to me after I leave the restroom. He say you, Robbie, are in trouble in the trees. I go with him, of course. But then he attacks me. He puts the tape on my mouth and my hands and makes me keep walking. Then he makes me sit and binds my feet, too."

"I wonder if he was trying to lure you, Robbie," Abe said.

"He must have been," I said. "But he lured you first."

"I'm afraid so. I never even saw him, and I don't know what he conked me out with. Dumb."

"I'd say *courageous*, myself," Lonnie offered.

"I sure am glad Robbie brought you along, man," Abe said. "We'd be toast otherwise."

I was glad, too. Because Queen Dumb would have been me heading into dark woods alone.

We walked without speaking for a few minutes. "You know, Chase only mentioned Pia," I said. "I bet that means someone else killed Sue."

"I imagine so." Abe tucked my arm through his and squeezed me close as an owl hoo-hooted in the distance.

Beth? Glen? Surely not Isaac. All I knew was that we'd had a close enough brush with death tonight to last a lifetime and a half.

Chapter Forty-eight

Twenty minutes later we sat in a comfortingly well-lit employee lunchroom, crowded around a rectangular table in the small space. Detective Henderson faced us, digital tablet at the ready. Beyond her on a counter sat a microwave, a big coffeepot, and a napkin dispenser. A fridge hummed at the end of the counter, and the air smelled like someone had burned popcorn not too long ago. Abe sat next to me, then Roberto and Maria, holding hands. Lonnie stood at the back.

Roberto retold his account of how he came to be taped up in the woods.

"What was it Mr. Broward told you to convince you to go with him?" Henderson asked. "What were his exact words?"

I cocked my head at Henderson. My father had just told her. Did she not believe him?

"He said my daughter is in the woods in some trouble. He made me believe she is there. So I go. Do you have a daughter, Detective?" He spread his hands.

"Actually, I do, sir." She smiled, but it was a pinched

smile. It sounded like she had some kind of problem with her daughter or was estranged from her.

"So you understand," Roberto continued. "Of course I go. Then he grab my hands, forces tape onto them. He tapes my mouth. We walk more. He makes me sit and tapes my feet. There is no daughter. He lied."

"Did he then stay there with you?" she asked

"No. He go away, then come back holding a big stick."

"What he hit me with, no doubt," Abe said. "I guess I was lucky he didn't tape me up, too."

Henderson looked at Lonnie. "Why did you enter the woods with Ms. Jordan? And did you note the time?"

"She asked me for help. I thought it was wise of her not to venture down the path alone." He glanced at me. "Had Broward tried to get you alone before?"

I thought back. "He didn't really get a chance. I haven't been alone that much this week. Although there were those sounds I heard in the night last night."

The detective nodded.

"What sounds were those?" Abe asked, his voice still hoarse.

"A metal-scratching-metal kind of sound. I sometimes wear earplugs to sleep, but I didn't last night. And I found marks on the lock plate on my back door this morning after I remembered the sounds."

"It probably won't surprise you that we weren't able to find any traceable evidence on your door, Ms. Jordan," Henderson said.

"So I guess he got desperate at shutting me up

directly, and figured he could lure me into trouble by using my father and my boyfriend as bait," I said.

Lonnie nodded. "She seemed very worried for her Italian father. At the entrance of the path she saw a piece of purple cloth she said was the kind of handkerchief Mr. O'Neill carries. We left it *in situ.*"

"Your car might have knocked it off, though," I said, remembering what a tight fit the SUV had been for the path.

Henderson tapped into her tablet.

Lonnie went on. "As for the timing, I radioed in my plan. The security office will have the time."

"So you and Ms. Jordan found Mr. O'Neill unconscious with a head wound. He awoke and jumped up to go farther into the woods?"

"I didn't exactly jump up, but I self-assessed," Abe said. "I'm a former military medic, and decided I didn't have a concussion and my balance was fine. I thought about safety in numbers, too. So I accompanied them to look for Roberto."

"Which of the three of you saw Mr. Fracasso first?" she asked.

"I did," I said. "Lonnie and Abe were scanning the edges of the clearing with their flashlights, and I saw my father's shoes." I smiled at him. *His very Italian leather shoes.*

"Then what happened?"

"I was ready to take the duct tape off his mouth when he looked really alarmed at something behind me. Abe was facing us, helping with his light. When I turned to look, Chase had snuck up behind Abe and put the wire around his neck." I shuddered, remembering the scene. "I yelled for Lonnie. Abe jabbed his light at Chase's face. In a second Lonnie hauled Chase off Abe and forced Chase to the ground."

Lonnie nodded slowly. "Correct."

"Did Mr. Broward speak at all?" the detective asked.

"He was livid with me. Said I had spoiled everything for him. That I'd been spying on him. Poking into his business."

"He said he'd been all set," Abe added. "Said Pia was out of the way, so he could focus on his campaign, except Robbie had interfered."

"Would that be his senatorial campaign?" Henderson poised her raised fingers above the tablet.

"I believe so," I said.

"So Mr. Dinnsen took down the attacker. Then what?"

"I unwound the wire from Abe. He cut the tape off Roberto's wrists and ankles. Lonnie taped up Chase. And he called you on my cell because his walkie-talkie was out of range."

Maria murmured something to Roberto. He addressed her in Italian for several minutes, and her expression grew increasingly horrified.

"May I see your wounds, please, Mr. O'Neill? I'd like photographic evidence."

Abe unwound the scarf and gingerly peeled back the handkerchief. In the hour since he'd been attacked, the hairline cut had stopped bleeding. Maria gasped and crossed herself at the sight. Henderson took out her phone and snapped a few shots, then came around behind him and took several pictures of the back of his head.

"You probably ought to have those wounds seen to," Henderson advised Abe.

"I will, thanks," he assured her.

"Deputy Bird has secured the suspect at our facility in Nashville," Henderson said.

Roberto translated. Maria nodded.

"Thank you," Maria said to Henderson. "Thank you."

"You should be thanking these people, not me, Ms. Fracasso. You can all rest safe now. But I'd discourage further nighttime walks in woods you are not familiar with." The last bit she directed at me.

"So you aren't thinking Chase also killed Sue?" I asked.

"That is our current position, yes." The detective stood, put away her tablet, and sighed. "If you'll excuse me, I still have a second murderer to track down."

I followed her out into the hall. "One more thing, Detective?"

She turned. Up close I could see how tired she looked, how the skin around her eyes was strained. "Yes?"

I kept my voice soft. "I ran into Paula Berry at the festival earlier tonight. That is, she and her father had made a short appearance on the main stage. Glen said they were going to start a scholarship in Sue's name to help a needy young musician come to the festival every year. Then he kind of broke down, and Paula asked for the public's help in solving the crime."

"The second part I am aware of."

"Well, I literally bumped into her later while I was looking for my father. She'd been drinking, and she told me she didn't think her father loved Sue. And didn't like her, either. For what it's worth."

The detective regarded me. "Such information regarding their relationship is new to me. I'll take it under advisement. Did you have anything else?"

"No. Except . . . thank you for working on these cases."

Henderson lifted a shoulder and dropped it. "We were getting pretty close to Broward. Sorry you had to bear the brunt of his attack."

"Hey, all's well that ends well, right?" It was one of Adele's favorite phrases.

"I'll be a lot happier when the second homicide case has ended well, too. And we're not there yet. Thank you for being forthcoming, Ms. Jordan." She turned and strode down the hall.

Chapter Forty-nine

I could barely pry my eyes open the next morning. I hadn't done a lick of prep last night because we'd arrived home so late. I'd set my alarm for five o'clock to compensate. When I got my eyelids wide enough open to see the clock, I was instantly awake. It read six-thirty. *Gah*. I was in big trouble.

Abe had decided not to go to the ER last night. Instead, we carefully cleaned his injured neck, and he had me pat clean the back of his head with hydrogen peroxide. He'd spread a thin layer of antibiotic ointment on the narrow neck cut. Then we'd both fallen into a deep sleep. I had no idea how he had roused himself at his usual early hour without waking me, but he was definitely gone.

My gaze fell on a note addressed to me next to the clock. I leaned over and unfolded it.

Let you sleep in. No worries in the kitchen.
I'm off to check in at work and hope to be
released home to rest.
Love, Abe.

I wrinkled my nose. No worries? With customers due to arrive in half an hour, I wasn't sure how I wasn't supposed to worry. I hurriedly washed up and dressed. I pulled my hair back, laced up my work tennies, and dashed food into Birdy's bowl.

When I opened the door to the store, I froze. And sniffed. And smiled. The air was redolent with the fragrance of coffee, the perfume of sizzling sausage, the aroma of biscuits baking. Danna worked the stove and Turner had set all the tables, stocked the caddies, and straightened the chairs.

"Am I dreaming?" I asked. I heard Birdy reply so I quickly locked the door to the apartment before he could sneak in.

Danna laughed. "We thought we'd let you sleep in a little for once."

"Did Abe put you up to this?"

"Not really," Turner said. "Coffee?"

"Bless your fabulous heart." I sank into a chair and watched the machinery of my helpers run like it had been freshly oiled.

Danna brought me a piping hot mug. "My mom got a report you'd captured that awful man. She heard Abe was hurt, and you and Roberto almost were. So I called Turner and we came over really early to help out. Abe saw us when he was leaving, and he went back in and left you a note."

My throat thickened with the thoughtful gesture. I took her hand and squeezed it in both of mine. "I can't thank you both enough. Is there anything left to do?"

"Just have your coffee." Danna extricated her hand.

"We might get kind of a flood of people who are going to be curious about what happened. We'll have plenty of work for all three of us once we open."

How did I get so lucky?

"Danna, have you heard from Isaac? Is he all right?" Was I really asking if he'd been arrested, too?

She gave me a thumbs-up. "He's good. Spent the night at home. Went into the state park to work today. The detective seems to be leaving him alone for now."

"I'm glad to hear it."

Turner pulled out two pans of biscuits and slid in two more. Danna returned to the grill and moved sausages and bacon around. I finished my coffee, carried the mug to the sink, and slid an apron over my head. I grabbed a biscuit and a piece of bacon so I wouldn't run out of steam in the next few hours until the lull. When seven o'clock hit, I was ready. I headed for the door to unlock it and turned the sign to OPEN.

We had the usual assortment of locals and festival-goers who kept us on our toes for the next two hours. And sure enough, every once in a while somebody would ask about the excitement last night.

The latest was a pair of South Lick women who always came in together. "Heared you captured an-other killer last night, Robbie. Good for you," one said, her eyes bright with what she must perceive as proximity to a hero.

"Not exactly," I protested. "But I understand the sheriff's detective does have someone in custody."

"The bad guy was staying right upstairs, wasn't

he?" the other asked. "Weren't you afraid you'd be killed in your bed?"

I winced. "No, frankly I wasn't. Can I get you ladies anything else this morning?" When they said no, I left them their check and moved on.

I took a quick break to text Abe. Thanks for the sleep-in. Hope you're not hurting too much. Did they let you off?

He didn't reply right away. He could be home sleeping, or maybe the workload was urgent and they'd asked him to put in a full shift, after all. After last night, I was nervous Sue's killer would go after him for reasons I couldn't even guess. It was a dangerous world out there, as we'd been shown only a scant ten hours earlier. I turned my back on the bustling restaurant and pressed his number.

It rang. And rang. And rang some more. I was about to disconnect when a sleepy Abe said, "Mornin', Robbie."

I wasn't sure I'd ever felt so relieved. "I'm just checking up on you. Sounds like you were sleeping."

"I was. Boss told me to go home and heal."

"Good advice. Your door is locked, right?"

"Locked up tight. Don't worry. I'll be fine, sweetheart."

My eyes filled. I blinked away the emotion and sniffed.

"Hey, are you crying?" he asked. "Didn't I say I'd be fine?"

"You did. And I'm glad." Behind me Danna dinged the READY bell. Silverware clattered and bacon sputtered. "I better get back to the breakfast rush. Give me a call when you wake up, okay?"

"You got it. Love you."

"Love you," I whispered in return. I took a deep breath and faced my restaurant again.

By nine-thirty when Adele came in a couple of tables had freed up. She made a beeline for me and enveloped me in a hug to top all hugs.

"Hey, I can't breathe," I told her after a full minute.

She held me at arm's length. "I can't decide if I'm so proud of you I could bust, or if I want to slap you upside the head. A little bit of both, I spose. Going and getting yourself all tangled up with criminals again. I declare, Roberta Jordan." She shook her head, and then hugged me again. When she let me go, she sniffed and swiped at both eyes. "Look at me, I'm turning into a sentimental old fool."

"Hey, you know I love you any way you turn," I said, my own eyes filling in return.

Turner dinged the READY bell and Danna had her arms full of dirty dishes.

"Go sit down and I'll bring you coffee." I kissed Adele's lined cheek, as soft as new flannel.

I delivered four breakfasts, poured Adele coffee, and looked up to see Roberto and Maria approach.

Adele jumped to her feet. "You two set right here with me. I'm glad we get one more chance to visit. You're heading home today, am I right?"

"Yes, we are," my father affirmed.

"It's been real good to see you both," Adele said. "You come back any old time."

"We come back," Maria said.

"Did you sleep well?" I asked her as Roberto pulled out a chair for her at Adele's table.

"Yes, *grazie a Dio.*"

"Good." I kissed my father's cheek—not soft like Adele's, but freshly shaven and smelling like rainwater from the aftershave he always wore—and said I'd get them both coffee. By the time I got back, Buck had come in and ambled up to their table.

"Good morning, Buck." I did not kiss him on the cheek, but I did take a second look. His expression was far more somber than usual. "Looks like you have some bad news."

"Welp, it's good and it's bad. Mind if I set down?" he asked Adele.

"Please. Then tell us what's up."

Buck glanced at me, his eyebrows up in a hopeful look.

I laughed. "Yes, I'll bring you coffee and order up your usual breakfast. Don't start until I'm back."

I asked Danna to make him one of nearly everything, grabbed a mug and the coffeepot, and headed over to hear Buck's news.

"It's this way." He spoke softly so as not to broadcast to the whole restaurant. "Our esteemed sheriff's detective made another arrest real early this morning in the case of Ms. Berry's homicide."

"But that's got to be good, right?" I asked, puzzled.

"Yes, ma'am. That's good. Problem is, Detective Henderson came into possession of evidence indicating Glen Berry was the perpetrator of the crime."

I sucked in breath, focusing on him.

"Yep, he up and killed his own sweet wife. Local businessman and all. It's a crying shame."

Voices had hushed around us. Buck hadn't kept his voice as low as he'd hoped. Customers glanced over and then away, and a new buzz of excited discussion swelled and grew. I felt eyes on us from behind me, too, and saw Danna and Turner looking our way.

"Well, I never," Adele said with a sorrowful head shake. "Leaving that poor Paula as good as an orphan, too."

Paula, who had been deadly correct last night regarding her father's lack of love for Sue.

"He sure put on a good show of grieving for Sue," I said, thinking back, even to his performance last evening at the park.

"Some of the best criminals do, Robbie." Buck poured a half cup of sugar into his coffee and stirred. "Heck, some murderers might as well get nominated for one of them Oscars, they're that good of actors."

Roberto spoke softly in Italian to Maria. "What was the evidence?" he asked Buck.

"Seems the couple who found Sue's body the other morning saw a car driving away," Buck said. "Later they saw another vehicle with the Berry liquor store bumper sticker and they recognized it. Turns out there are traces of blood in the car, too. It isn't all Anne has, but it put the final nail in the coffin for Glen Berry."

"So to speak," Adele said.

I kept picturing my murder puzzle. All the names, all the possibilities. "And Beth Ferguson is off the hook for both crimes."

Buck nodded. "That she is."

"Isaac, too," I added, glancing Danna's way.

"Isaac, too," Buck confirmed.

Detective Henderson had to be happy about a second *All's well that ends well* in as many days. I knew I was.

Recipes

FRIED APPLES

Danna and Robbie prepare fried apples as a special to celebrate the bluegrass festival.

INGREDIENTS
½ cup butter, cubed
6 medium unpeeled tart red apples, sliced
¾ cup sugar
¾ teaspoon ground cinnamon

DIRECTIONS
Melt butter in a large cast-iron or other oven-proof skillet. Add apples and ½ cup sugar; stir to mix well. Cover and cook over low heat for 20 minutes or until apples are tender, stirring frequently. Add remaining sugar and cinnamon. Cook and stir over medium-high heat 5 to 10 minutes longer.

ASIAN SPICY SESAME NOODLE SALAD

Turner re-creates a dish he ate at a restaurant for a lunch special. Robbie also takes it to widower Glen Berry as a condolence offering.

INGREDIENTS
1 package soba or rice noodles
2 tablespoons sesame oil
1 tablespoon soy sauce
1 tablespoon sugar
4 tablespoons unflavored rice vinegar
Dash red pepper flakes
1 sweet red pepper, diced
1 cucumber, peeled and diced
1 cup snow or snap peas, trimmed and sliced
     lengthwise

DIRECTIONS
Boil noodles according to directions on package. Drain, toss with one tablespoon sesame oil, and let cool.

In a serving bowl, whisk together the rest of the oil with the soy sauce, sugar, vinegar, and pepper flakes. Add the noodles and prepared vegetables and toss. Adjust seasonings to taste.

Serve chilled or at room temperature.

JANE CARTER'S SUGAR CREAM PIE

A Hoosier favorite, this recipe is kindly shared by Jane Carter. Robbie makes the pies for her restaurant customers.

INGREDIENTS
1 stick butter
1 scant cup sugar
¼ cup cornstarch
2 cups milk
½ cup half-and-half
¼ teaspoon salt
1 teaspoon vanilla
Cinnamon
1 pre-baked and cooled piecrust (either homemade from your favorite recipe or obtained at the store)

DIRECTIONS
In a medium-sized saucepan, melt butter, sugar, and cornstarch, stirring to dissolve. Add milk, half-and-half, salt, and vanilla. Cook until thick, stirring constantly.

Pour into prepared crust and sprinkle with cinnamon. Chill at least two hours before serving.

KAHLÚA BROWNIE ICE CREAM SANDWICHES

Phil makes these for the lunch dessert special.

INGREDIENTS
Kahlúa brownies (recipe in *Flipped for Murder*)
1 quart vanilla or coffee ice cream
Aluminum foil, cut into eight-inch squares

DIRECTIONS
Remove ice cream from freezer to soften slightly.
Cut cooled brownies into three-inch squares, then
slice crosswise with a sharp knife. If the knife sticks,
dip it in water before cutting.

Spread a scoop of ice cream a quarter inch thick
on bottom half of brownie. Cover with top, wrap in
foil, and place in freezer. Repeat for all brownies.

CHICKEN WITH WINE-MUSHROOM SAUCE

Maria enjoys this dish at Hoosier Hollow restaurant.

INGREDIENTS
2 tablespoons butter
1 pound boneless and skinless chicken breasts,
    cut in half lengthwise
Salt and pepper to taste
1 medium onion, chopped
12 ounces white mushrooms sliced
3 cloves garlic, minced
1 tablespoon all-purpose flour
¼ cup white wine
1½ cups half-and-half
¼ cup minced parsley

DIRECTIONS
Add the butter to a large skillet and melt over medium high heat.

Season chicken breasts on both sides with salt and pepper. Place chicken breasts in skillet and cook on both sides, about 5 minutes per side or until no longer pink inside. Remove chicken from skillet and keep warm.

Reduce heat to medium. Add onion to skillet and cook for a couple minutes until onion is translucent and soft. Add mushrooms and stir. Season mushrooms generously with salt and pepper. Cook about 5 minutes, stirring occasionally. Add garlic and cook for another minute. Sprinkle the flour over the onions, mushrooms, and garlic, and stir. Add wine and cook off the wine for a couple more minutes.

Add half-and-half and cook 3 minutes, stirring occasionally or until sauce reduces a bit and thickens. Return chicken to the skillet and integrate with the sauce.

Garnish with parsley and serve hot over rice, pasta, or buttered potatoes.

Connect with

Us

Visit us online at
KensingtonBooks.com
to read more from your favorite authors, see books
by series, view reading group guides, and more.

for sneak peeks, chances to win books and prize packs,
and to share your thoughts with other readers.

facebook.com/kensingtonpublishing
twitter.com/kensingtonbooks

Tell us what you think!

To share your thoughts, submit a review,
or sign up for our eNewsletters, please visit:
KensingtonBooks.com/TellUs.